Until Eyes ARE MINE

An Until You Novel

Book Two

D.M. DAVIS

Copyright © 2018 D.M. Davis
Until You Are Mine
Until You series by D.M. Davis

ISBN13: 978-0-9997176-3-9
Published by D.M. Davis

www.dmckdavis.com

Cover Design by Hang Le
Editing by Tamara Mataya
Proofreading by Mountains Wanted Publishing & Indie Author Services
Formatting by Champagne Book Design

This is a work of fiction. Names, places, characters and incidents are the product of the author's imagination and are fictitious. Any resemblance to actual persons, living or dead, events or establishments is solely coincidental.

This story contains mature themes, strong language, and sexual situations. It is intended for adult readers.

Playlist

Say Hey (I Love You) by Michael Franti & Spearhead

Little Things by One Direction

Birthday Cake by Rhianna

Let me Love You by DJ Snake (featuring Justin Bieber)

Birthday Sex by Jeremiah

Then There's You by Charlie Puth

I Get to Love You by Ruelle

Kindly Calm Me Down by Meghan Trainor

I Miss you by Adele

Mercy by Sean Mendes

This Town by Niall Horan

She Will Be Loved by Maroon 5

When reality becomes too much, dream of a better future.

This is for all the dreamers looking for more than they have and
daring to reach for it. It's never too late to ask for more.
To expect more. To strive for more.
It's *never* too late.

Until You
ARE MINE

Sometimes you have to leap
Before you now if you can fly

PART 1

HAZE

MARCH

One

Samantha

WEEKS PASS IN AN EMOTIONAL HAZE. THE NEVER-ending stream of friends and strangers dropping in to pay their respects by bringing food or flowers has long stopped. It's just me and Mom now. Except, it truly feels like it's just me and a body that used to be my mother. She barely leaves her room. She's not handling Dad's death well. I can't blame her. I really can't, but she can't spend the rest of her life in bed. She needs to feed, bathe, and clothe herself.

It's like I've lost my mother too. Like I'm the mother, having to remind her of life's basic needs.

It's hard getting myself up and to school when most days I would rather just roll over and go back to sleep. Besides missing my dad, I miss Jace and Joseph. I miss Joseph oh so much, but I just can't go there. The immediacy of life is banging down my door, far too many things to worry about and stress over to think about Joseph and our future that may never be.

The reality is, I'm barely keeping it together. I'm in my senior year of high school, getting ready to graduate, intern at MCI this summer, and start at UT in the fall while also trying to keep our house running like my father was here. Like his absence hasn't left me with paying bills, keeping track of home and car maintenance, grocery shopping, dealing with the bank and lawyers to sort out my father's estate. Things an eighteen-year-old should not have to deal with.

There's that, too. Today's my eighteenth birthday.

I'm not up to celebrating. There doesn't seem much to celebrate. Really, it's just another day. I've had to make an effort to be alone today. I changed my shift at work. I told Margot I was spending my birthday with my mom in a quiet celebration, no fanfare. Margot was disappointed, but I knew she understood why I didn't invite her to come over.

Then there was the text from Joseph. He asked what I was doing to celebrate, and I told him I was going out with Margot. He's been texting me every day. He wants to move back to where we were, and I'm trying to move forward without him. Most days, I don't answer. I can't give him or me false hope. Although the last thing I want is to be apart from him, my self-preservation says I should close the book on Joseph, since he slept with someone else three minutes after we broke up. I try not to think about him having sex with that woman. He doesn't mention it, and because I don't respond most of the time, it goes unaddressed.

What is there to say, really? I broke up with him. I have no right to be upset or jealous. I made my bed. Now I'm lying in it alone, trying not to think about who's been sharing his bed for the past two weeks.

Jace and Michael were my last loose ends on the whole birthday lie. I spoke to Jace a few days ago, telling him I was going out with Margot. He's been so distant lately, he really didn't take much convincing. I think he only asked out of obligation anyway. I don't think he really cares, not anymore. As for Michael, he told me he was going to be out of town but to save him a piece a birthday cake, and he'd see me tomorrow. There's always the stream of federal agents watching me, but they couldn't care less if it's my birthday.

My mom, well, she never mentioned it. I doubt she even realizes what day it is. I made her dinner and actually got her to eat in the kitchen with me. We ate in silence. I tried to smile and keep things light, but I'm just not feeling it. Today of all days, I shouldn't have to pretend things are fine, that my dad's death isn't taking a horrible toll on our lives.

Dad would be so disappointed to see us now, to see how far we've fallen from the happy family we used to be.

When Mom escapes to her room, I clean up the kitchen. After the last dish is put away, I pull out the single piece of cheesecake I brought home from work yesterday, slide it onto a plate and grab a fork.

I stare at it. Its top is bare, no birthday writing to wish me *Happy 18th Birthday, Sam.* No flickering candle for me to wish on before the wax drips down.

I wish...

What would I wish?

Impossible wish? For my father to still be alive.

Improbable wish? For my father's killer to be caught and for Joseph to show up at my door begging me to take him back.

Realistic wish? I think maybe I've had enough of reality.

I glance around the empty kitchen. No friends and family to sing me happy birthday and *many more...*

Who would have thought last year would have been my last happy birthday? If I had known, I would have made a better wish—the impossible wish—for time to stand still—for my father to still be alive.

I place the cheesecake back in the fridge. Maybe I'll eat it later, after I finish my homework. I turn off all the lights and pass through the quiet hall to the library, seeking comfort in the room I love, filled with books and possibilities of escape.

A few hours later, I indulge in a long soak in the bathtub. I don't do it often, but since being shot, hot baths soothe the ache in my shoulder better than most things.

About the time I'm ready to slip into bed, my phone rings. *Darn, I forgot to turn it off.*

I answer instead of ignoring it like I really want to.

"What the fuck, Sam?" Jace barks into the phone.

"Hi, Jace. How are you?" I say calmly, trying to delay the brewing conflict.

"I was fine until I got a call from Joe asking me why you didn't go out with Margo for your birthday."

"How does he know I didn't go out with Margot? And why's he calling you?" *It's not like you give a shit.*

"He called to see if I knew what your plans were and if they'd changed."

"Oh." That still doesn't answer how Joseph knew.

"Why didn't you go out with Margot?"

I sit on my bed, peering out the window, my heart beating in my ears.

"Sam?" he says softly.

"Yeah?" My voice tightens with emotion.

"Shit, don't cry." He exhales a deep breath.

"I'm sorry." I fall back on my bed, wiping my eyes.

"Spill." He's still pissed.

"Why are you mad? It's my birthday. Aren't I allowed to spend it as I want to?" I ask defensively.

"You mean, like *it's my party, and I'll cry if I want to* kind of crap?"

"Yes, exactly like that."

"Did you?" His voice is losing its edge.

"Did I what?"

"Sam. Did you cry on your birthday, alone?"

"These days, crying on my birthday, or any other day, is not much of a stretch."

"What's going on, Sam?" His concern is clear, but it's too little too late.

I sigh and sit up. "Nothing's going on, Jace."

"That's bullshit, and you know it. Talk to me."

"Are you mad because I lied, or are you mad because you've been inconvenienced in having to call and check up on me? I must be cutting into your fucking time."

"Sam." My name is full of regret, yet I'm not sure if it's for calling him on his shit or because I've hit the truth—he'd rather be fucking than talking to his kid sister.

I rub my forehead and squeeze my eyes shut, trying to relieve some discomfort from my growing headache. "You know what? I'm going to stretch my newly liberated eighteen-year-old wings and utilize my right to not talk. I love you, but I'm hanging up now."

4

He yells as I end the call.

A beat passes, and my phone rings. Does he really think I'm going to answer when I just hung up on him?

A second later, my phone chimes with a voicemail. Then a text:

Jace: *Answer the damn phone!*

Me: *I don't want to talk.*

Jace: *Too fucking bad, answer your PHONE!*

My phone rings again. I reject it.

Jace: *Sam, come on. Talk to me.*

Me: *Nope. Don't you have some tail to chase? Stretch your manwhore wings.*

Jace: *HARSH, Sam. Harsh.*

When I don't answer on his third and fourth calls, he gives up.

A few minutes later my phone rings—Joseph. It will be the same conversation. He doesn't need to get involved. I send his call, and the two that follow, to voicemail. Then he resorts to texting:

Joseph: *Sam, please talk to me. You're worrying me.*

Apparently Jace didn't give up—he just sicced Joseph on me.

Me: *I don't want to talk. I'm fine. Don't worry. Leave me alone for a while.*

Joseph: *What does that mean? …a while?*

Me: *It means, IT'S MY FUCKING BIRTHDAY AND I CAN SPEND IT ALONE IF I WANT TO AND I DON'T HAVE TO EXPLAIN IT TO YOU OR ANYBODY ELSE. See? You should have left me alone. Not a good time. Just let me be for a couple of days.*

Joseph: *Not fucking happening!*

Me: *You don't have a choice. You're not my father. You're not even my boyfriend. Go with Jace and find some college girls to fuck. I'm turning my phone off now. Bye.*

I turn my phone off and turn the ringer off on the house phone in the kitchen. There are other phones in the house I hear ringing in the background, but I ignore them. The phone in Mom's room is always off these days, so they can call all they like.

5

I'm sure I'll regret my texts and lies over the past few days. But at the moment, I just can't. I don't have it in me to be strong and act like everything is okay, because you know what? It fucking is *not* okay! Not by a long shot.

I turn off all the lights and climb in bed, trying to focus on the things I can control, which seems like so little at the moment.

Samantha

The doorbell startles me awake Wednesday morning—early, but not so early I shouldn't already be up for school. Did I forget to set my alarm? I roll to my back and consider just letting whoever it is exhaust their efforts and go the hell away.

The persistent ringing turns into persistent knocking and then pounding. If they haven't woken my mom, they will surely have woken the neighbors by now.

I scurry out of bed, don a robe, and tiptoe down the stairs. Why am I being so quiet? There's no way they could hear me through all that racket they're making.

I creep to the front door. The doorbell chimes again. I jump and nearly scream, but manage to keep it together so whoever's on the other side of the door doesn't hear me.

I take a deep breath to calm my racing heart, and look through the peephole.

Fin and Joseph.

Shit!

I silently bang my forehead against the door.

"Go away," I say to the crack in the door so I don't have to raise my voice.

"Samantha." Joseph's voice is muffled, but there is no way I could mistake the way he says my name for anyone else.

Fin chimes in. "Is that any way to greet us?"

"No, it's not. I'm sorry, but I don't want to talk." *And I most definitely don't want to see you.*

Silence.

I don't look through the peephole. I don't need to see them to know the cogs in their brains are clicking as they think of a way to get me to open the door, which I'm sure I'll end up doing. I can't be mean to them in person.

"How about this?" Fin offers. "You open the door. Let us in so we can truly see you are, in fact, alright. You don't have to talk to us. You don't have to say a word if you don't want to."

I peer out at them. "Not happening. You need to go. Joe, you should be at school. Fin, you have a company to run. You shouldn't be here. What's happening with me is none of your concern."

"The fuck it isn't." Joseph pounds the door. "Open this goddamn door right now!"

I actually laugh, he's so angry. To see him here in the middle of the week when he should be in Austin, and knowing he's this upset is wrongly satisfying and quite gratifying, to say the least.

"If you don't leave, I'm going to call the cops," I warn.

"That won't be necessary." Michael steps into view.

Fucking Michael.

"I'm surprised you didn't just break in like you did last time, Michael."

Joseph's head whips around to glare at Michael. *Whoa, Joseph's not happy about that.*

Michael smiles deviously. "I have a key, actually." He holds it up to the peephole. "I don't need to break in anymore."

"Then why all the pounding and racket? You've disturbed the whole neighborhood."

Displeased, he narrows his eyes at Fin and Joseph. "I just got here. Believe me, I would have handled this differently if these two schmucks hadn't beaten me here." I swear his eyes lock on mine, knowing I'm looking at him. "Now, open the door, Sam. Or I'll use my key. Your choice."

Damn. Damn. Damn. *Fucking Michael.*

I'm going to regret this. I know it.

I unlock the door. Instead of opening it, I race up the stairs trying to escape them.

Joseph's voice stops me at the top. "You'd better be going to get dressed," he warns. "You've got five minutes, and then I'm coming in there and will drag you down here to talk to us in whatever *state of dress* you're in."

My mouth falls open, and I scowl at Michael, who smiles unabashedly. "I told you he wouldn't like me seeing you in your t-shirt and panties."

"Asshole," I sneer.

He laughs and shakes his head. "You have no idea, princess."

"Michael," Joseph barks.

Michael nods and motions to Fin. They disappear into the den.

"Samantha." Joseph's voice is silky smooth, the voice I've come to know so well.

I clutch the railing as I peer down on him in his black t-shirt and jeans. Sexy as sin and as heartbreaking as ever.

"I'm serious, Samantha. Five minutes, then I'm coming to get you."

The sadness in his eyes painfully tightens my throat. I couldn't even reply if I tried.

I nod once and turn away, slamming my hand over my mouth as a sob tries to break free. *I can't do this. I can't be this close to him and not be affected by him.*

"Samantha."

The pain I saw in his eyes a moment ago is now in his voice. It pins me in place just before I manage to escape into my room. I don't know how he made it up the stairs so quickly and silently.

I wipe my tears. My face tipped down, I glance sideways over my left shoulder, hoping I'm in shadow enough to hide my tears. I remain silent.

"Please don't walk around barely dressed in front of Michael or anyone else."

Jesus. Seriously? Such a caveman. Then don't go sticking your dick in other women! I want to scream at him. But I don't. I simply nod and move toward my door.

He clasps my left shoulder, stopping my progress.

"Don't." I shrug to dislodge his hand as if it burns me.

I move past my doorway, slamming it behind me just as he says, "Samantha, please."

I only make it a few feet before I collapse into a mass of tears.

Please, God. Give me strength.

The door opens. "Christ, Sweetness." His footfall alerts me to his movement a second before he wraps me in his arms and lifts me off the floor.

I jerk violently. "Let me go, Joe. Dammit, let me go!"

His grip is firm as he carries me to my bed. "Never, Samantha. Never."

I beat at his chest, pleading with him. "Let me down."

"No." He squeezes me tightly as if he's afraid I'll disappear.

We drop to the bed.

"Jesus Christ. Stop!" He pins my arms beside my head and uses his body to stifle mine. "You're going to hurt your shoulder. Please stop fighting me." His chiseled face is stricken with anguish. "Please, Samantha."

His pleading breaks me.

I stop struggling. "If you ever cared for me, Joe. If you ever felt anything for me, please just let me go. Leave and don't look back."

The tears I've been fighting break free. I can't fight them anymore. I can't fight *him* anymore. He has to choose to leave. I can't make him, because deep down I don't want him to. I want him to stay and fight—for me—for us.

"Sweetness, it's because I do care, I'll never walk away from you. I could never leave you hurting like this." He releases his hold and wraps his arms around my back, burying his head in my neck, his entire body cocooning mine. "I'm sorry. I'm so fucking sorry." His voice cracks with anguish. "You have no idea how sorry I am. Please, please forgive me. Let me be here for you. Let me help you." He's crying. He's fucking crying.

Jesus. He's so perfect for me, it hurts to know it'll never be.

With little hesitation, I wrap my arms around him, squeezing him tightly. We hold each other as we expel all we've been through these past weeks, finding the comfort we both desperately need. Sorrow rolls off us in waves, deeply ravaging regret so palpable it's hard to breathe.

Eventually, our tears dry. He rolls to his back, taking me with him to lie alongside him. He kisses my forehead, then clears his throat and rasps, "Please stop calling me *Joe*. It's like a fucking knife to the gut every time you say it."

I knew it would bother him, rub him the wrong way. I get a small amount of pleasure in that. However, it's also a means to distance myself from him, protect my heart, or what's left of it. "I'll think about it."

He squeezes me, running his hand down my arm. "Well, think about it good and hard, because the next time you call me *Joe*, I'm going to take you in my arms and kiss, lick, and suck every inch of your body until you agree to call me *Joseph*."

Holy smokes, this man. My heart will never survive my traitorous body, which wants nothing more than for him to do all of that and more.

"Are you throwing down a gauntlet?" I tease, amazed by how easy it always is between us, at least when we're in person.

His chest ripples with his laugh. "No, Sweetness. I'm making you a promise. The first of many I intend to keep."

Two

Joseph

"WHY ARE YOU HERE, JOE?"

Fuck. She's gonna test me. Should I have expected less? I roll off the bed, pushing down my agitation, shaking my head. "I'm going to give you that one, but that's the last one." I bend down, hovering over her, looking into the amazing blue eyes I've missed so much. "The next time you call me *Joe*, I'm going to make good on my promise."

A wicked smile lights up her face, which should delight me, but it doesn't. She's not taking me seriously.

"You realize your promise is much more of an enticement than a deterrent, don't you?"

"I'm not playing games, Samantha. This is my heart we're talking about." I take her hand and hold it over my pounding heart. "You're in here, Samantha, and I'm not letting you go." I sit on the bed next to her and place my hand over her heart. "I need you to let me back in here, and you'll never do that as long as you're calling me *Joe*."

Her smirk is gone and replaced with the sadness consuming much of her life now.

"I know we have things to talk about. I know you still need time to process what I did and time to forgive me, and I'm going to wait that out. But, I'm not going to allow you to put an extra wall between us. That wall that says *I'm just some old Joe* to you. I'm not *Joe* to you. I'm

Joseph. Your Joseph. I need you to respect that and call me by that name. The rest I'll be patient for, but that, I will not stand for."

Her eyes cloud with unsaid emotions and desire. She may not admit it, but she likes it when I go all caveman on her. She might even crave it, need it. Her needs have been ignored for so long, she eats up the attention and my need to claim her—to be claimed by her.

I kiss her forehead and step away from the bed. "You need to get dressed." At the door, I glance back before opening it. "I'll be downstairs. Don't take too long, or I *will* come back and get you."

Leaving her on the bed, staring after me, I follow the scent of bacon into the kitchen to find Michael cooking and Fin sitting at the island drinking a cup of coffee. I head to the coffeemaker.

"Have y'all seen Eleanor?" I blow across my mug, then taking a tentative sip.

Michael glances at me before returning his focus to the eggs he's scrambling. "She's in her room, probably still in bed. Where she always is," he says flatly.

An arched brow from Fin gets my attention before I look back to Michael. "What do you mean *always?*"

Turning the stove off, he pushes the pan to the back burner and covers it before facing us. "She spends all of her time in her room. Sam ensures she eats and showers every day, but other than that, she's pretty much a lump of useless flesh."

"Jesus, Michael," Fin castigates.

Michael runs his fingers through his short buzz of brown hair. "It's harsh, I know. But the reality is, she's not functioning. She's not taking care of Sam. She's not working. She's not taking care of the house or any other matters Daniel handled. She's lost in her grief, and Sam's paying the price. She didn't even remember Sam's birthday, for fuck's sake."

"It's okay she didn't remember," Samantha's soft voice trails from the kitchen doorway.

"Fuck," Michael exclaims. "I'm sorry, Sam. I shouldn't have said that stuff."

"Or at least said it with a little more tact," Fin interjects.

I pull her into the kitchen and hand her a cup of coffee with cream and sugar, just the way she likes it. "Is it true though, Samantha? Is she really that bad?"

"It's...she's..." She sighs, her frustration palpable.

I lean down and kiss her head. "Hey, there's no judgment here. We just want to help."

She nods. "Yes, it's bad. I'm doing the best I can, which obviously is not enough if the three of you are here during the day when you should be working or at school."

The grandfather clock in the hall chimes eight times. "Shit! *I* should be at school." Samantha jumps.

I put my hand on her shoulder. "Stop. You're not going to school today. In fact, I think you should take the rest of the week off." I nod to Fin. "We'll talk to your principal and square it with him."

Fin exits the kitchen, understanding my silent request to call her school. He established a relationship with her principal while she was in the hospital. I was too preoccupied with her to even think of her school work.

Michael, ever the voice of reason—not always calm, but always reasonable— suggests we continue this conversation over breakfast. We agree and sit down to eat in the breakfast nook.

Fin joins us shortly with a silent nod, confirming her school situation has been handled. He sits at the table, surveying the kitchen. "The place looks clean, organized, better than the last time I saw it. It was a mess after the reception."

Sam glances at him, but doesn't say anything.

"How many times a week does the maid come?" Fin continues.

Samantha leans back in her chair. "Never."

"You've been doing all the cooking and cleaning?" I ask.

"Yes."

Fin grunts in appreciation. "Well, you're doing a good job. I'd hire you, if I didn't know you have higher aspirations."

She sets down her fork and scans the three of us. "Why don't y'all just ask me what you really want to know instead of going on this fishing expedition? It will probably save us a bunch of time and allow you to get back to your own lives faster."

I reach over and squeeze her hand. "We're not in any hurry. We're here to help, but we do need some details so we can be sure we're helping in the best way possible. Tell us what's going on with the house, and don't leave any details out."

Reluctantly, she fills us in on where things stand. She's been paying the bills, grocery shopping, etc. out of her savings account. She's also been cleaning, doing laundry, and managing the yard work and pool maintenance. I'm sure there's more, but that's all she's sharing at the moment.

"Christ. You should have told someone. Asked for help," I spout.

She just shakes her head. "Who was I supposed to dump all this on? There's no one. Just me."

"There's me, Fin, Michael, Jace. My entire family," I offer.

"It's not your responsibility. You all have busy lives. I can't burden you with this. And Jace can't handle this stuff from Austin. Plus, well, it isn't his forte, nor does he seem to be in a place to offer much help."

I can't disagree with the Jace assessment.

"That may be all true, but the burden doesn't fall to you alone. Not anymore." I squeeze her hand, making sure she understands I'm serious.

This shit right here, this self-sacrificing is going to stop. Now.

The bottom line is she's a senior in high school, who will graduate with an associate's degree and probably a 5.0 GPA because of the difficulty of the classes she is carrying. She has enough going on, plus dealing with her own loss and grief around her father. She doesn't need to be running a household and taking care of her mother too.

"Let's take care of one thing at a time." I get up to refill everyone's coffee. "Your mom needs help. We can move her to my parents' home. My mom would be more than willing to take care of her. She misses having someone to pamper since I moved out years ago. It would be a good interim solution to more drastic measures. We can see how it goes and then reassess in a week or so."

I wait for the three of them to voice any objections, but none come. "Okay, agreed.

"As for the household maintenance and financials, I recommend we let the lawyers set up arrangements for your and Jace's finances and a property manager for running the house."

I look to Samantha for confirmation. "Agreed?"

She gives a soft, "Yes."

"I would like to speak to Samantha alone about the next piece. Fin, would you mind calling our parents and getting the ball rolling with the lawyers?"

"On it." He stands and strides out of the room.

"See you in a bit," I say to Michael as I guide Samantha out of kitchen and to the library.

Samantha

When I woke up this morning, I thought today would end like it did the night before, and the night before that, and the night before that. Endless nights of homework, house work, and nursemaid to my mother. Apparently, I was wrong.

I have no idea what Joseph wants to speak to me about, but it can't be good if he wants it to be done in private.

"I don't want you here alone in this big house. As much as I'd like to stay, it's just not a possibility. Plus, I still think I'd be too much of a distraction to be beneficial." He quickly gets to the point, but I can hear the smile in his voice when he continues. "Not to mention you'd be a distraction for me and my school work too."

"We're not an item anymore. It's not your place to take care of me any longer. I don't expect you or anyone else to upturn your life. You're worried, I understand, but I'll be fine here by myself. You're taking the added pressure off by getting my mom settled with your parents, and the house will be taken care of shortly. As for being alone, I am most of the time anyway. That's nothing new."

He grimaces as if he realizes how true that fact it. "I want you to stay at Fin's."

What? "Fin's?"

"Yes. You shouldn't be alone. He'll look out for you and keep you safe."

"Safe? I don't need Fin to keep me safe." I move away, pacing the room. "No. No. That's not happening." My mind races. I can't put them in danger. I have FBI protection all because my father's killer is still out there, seeking the information he unsuccessfully tried to squeeze out of my dad. The information he's willing to kill for. I can't knowingly put Joseph or anyone else in danger. The killer knows me, but I don't know for sure if he knows who's important to me. I'm not willing to take a chance on anyone else's life.

"Samantha." He moves to me, lifting me up in his arms.

"Put me down." It's more of a plea than an order.

"No, you're panicking." He sits on the nearest couch, holding me in his lap.

God, I love being in his lap, feeling his protective arms around me.

He cups my cheek, ensuring I meet his gaze. "I know why you broke up with me. You did it to protect me. And now you don't want to live with Fin because you think you'll put him in danger."

Shit.

"You're not in this alone, Sweetness. Michael and his team have been watching you for weeks, but I've also had Victor and his guys on you, as well."

"Joseph." What is he saying?

"You were never really alone. I was always there, watching, keeping you safe, and I will continue to do so. But, it'll be easier to do it in a high security building like MCI towers, where Fin and Matt live and work." His fingers slip into my hair as he pulls me closer. His lips press against my temple, breathing slowly and steadily.

His stillness centers me, and my panic begins to dissipate as I relax into him, matching his breathing, closing my eyes and feeling the sense of home he instills in me.

"I won't let anything happen to you or your family," he whispers.

I wrap my arms around him and bury my face in his neck. "It's you I worry about. If he wants to get to me, you're my weakness. That's why I pushed you away—not because I don't want you as much as I ever did."

His fingers gently move down to massage the back of my neck. "Sweetness, I appreciate you thinking breaking up with me would fix that, but I don't believe it does. The killer can't be that easily deceived. He would see through your ruse eventually, just as I did."

"You believed me at first." Seeing regret wash across his face and his demeanor change, I wish I could take back my words.

"Yes, I did. I was in hell believing you no longer wanted me. And I—"

"Stop." I push my way out of his lap, needing distance.

He reluctantly lets me go, but stands to pursue me, his face pained. "Samantha."

I can't take it. "No, we don't need to talk about this. I hurt you. I'm sorry for that. You have no idea how sorry or how bad it hurt me too." My fist beats against my chest. He'll never know how sorry I am for driving him into the arms of another woman. I swipe angrily at my tears. "But, we don't need to talk about the..." I wave my hand at him, trying to dispel the thoughts, "...the other stuff."

I back away as he continues to moves closer. "Baby, we do need to talk about it." He captures me around the waist, stopping my retreat.

I close my eyes and turn my head to the side. "Please, I can't. Not now." *Not ever.* The thought of him making love to another woman makes me nauseated all over again. I stumble back, hating my weakness, letting something I caused affect me so strongly. "Please," I say as much to him as to myself.

He pulls me into his arms. "Okay. Okay. Not now." He kisses my head. "But make no mistake, Sweetness, we will talk about it. I hurt you, and you need to give me a chance to make amends." He squeezes me tighter. "I need you to forgive me." His voice is heavy with emotion.

"There's—"

He cuts me off with a kiss. A soft, chaste kiss. "Shhh. No more." His lips return to mine, but this time they're no longer chaste, but hungry.

Wonderfully hungry.

Joseph's parents showed up a little over an hour ago. They're all treating me with kid gloves, like I might break. I won't, but I may go off on them and have another bout of emotions. So, I guess it's better they stay clear of me, or I stay clear of them.

I'm sitting at the top of the stairs. I was on my way to my room, but thought better of it, afraid they'd leave with my mom, and I wouldn't get a chance to say goodbye.

"Sam," Fin says from the bottom of the stairs. "Why are you sitting there?"

I shrug instead of answering him. I don't want to share my pathetic thoughts.

He climbs the stairs and sits sideways on the step below me. "I'm glad you're coming to stay with me. I didn't like the idea of you staying here alone."

"According to Joseph, I haven't really been alone."

He contemplates a moment before speaking. "Well, in some ways, no, but in other ways, you have been." He touches my arm. "You've *felt* alone, and we don't want you to feel that way anymore. This is a good compromise, and I get the added bonus of company too."

"I don't need a babysitter. I'm quite capable of taking care of myself." In my head, I sat up straight, and my words came out strong and with conviction. In reality, I'm slumped against the wall, and I think it came out more like a murmur.

"You are capable, and I'm not a babysitter." He moves to the top step and pulls me into his side. I don't have the energy to protest, and, frankly, I don't want to. "I'm a friend, and I think you could use one of those right now."

"Okay," I agree. There are so many reasons I should continue to fight this, but one rather handsome six and half feet of convincing man named Joseph is wedging his way back in. I'm not sure I have the heart to continue fighting on my own, so it would be nice to have Joseph and his family on my side—standing up for me—protecting me.

"I thought for sure you'd fight Joe on this. I had a whole speech planned out and everything." He seems disappointed.

"Did you have visual aids, graphs, and diagrams? 'Cause I'm a sucker for a good presentation."

"Smartass." He releases me just as Joseph rounds the corner.

He scowls when he sees us. "Are you packed, Samantha?"

My contrition is obvious. "No, sorry."

He comes up the stairs, stopping in front of us, eyeing Fin and his nearness to me. "Don't you have someplace to be, brother?"

Fin laughs, shaking his head as he rises to his feet. "Calm yourself, caveman." He winks at me. "I'll see you later for dinner at my place." He nods at Joseph with a pat on the back before trotting down the stairs.

"Come on, I'll help you pack." He offers me his hand and pulls me to my feet.

"Have you talked to Jace?" I ask as we walk down the hall to my room.

He visibly stiffens. "Fin's going to call him and fill him in."

That's odd. "Why?"

"Why what?" His hand touches the sensitive spot on my lower back, and he chuckles when I arch in response. "So sensitive." He's laughing, but his eyes look at me with yearning, like he missed me nearly as much as I missed him.

"Why is Fin calling Jace instead of you calling him?" I pull his hand away from my back, but don't release it.

19

"Why aren't you calling him and telling him yourself?" He side-steps my question.

"Because I'm mad at him, and I think he's mad at me. I really don't want to deal with him right now."

He nods and follows me into my closet, pulling down the suitcase I point out on the top shelf. He lays it out on my bed, unzipping it. "My answer is kind of the same. I'm not very happy with Jace at the moment, and it's probably best for all of us if Fin deals with him right now."

I touch his arm and wait for him to make eye contact. "Do I dare ask why?"

He gives a sad smile before cupping my nape and running his thumb across my jawline. "No, it's probably best you don't."

"Okay." I survey my room, thinking of where to start.

So, Joseph's idea of *helping me pack* is him lying on my bed, pe-rusing my panties and commenting on their lack of material. I swipe his latest acquisition out of his hand. "Joseph, are you trying to be the creepy guy who stalks my underwear drawer? 'Cause you're doing a fine impression of a creeper."

He holds up his hands up in surrender, sitting back against the headboard. "I am most definitely. *Not. That. Guy.*"

"Thank god. You were creeping me out. I was starting to think I'd turn around, and you'd be wearing a pair of my panties."

He chuckles. "Sweetness, my junk wouldn't fit in that scrap of ma-terial you call panties."

I can't help but laugh. "So, you're not saying you wouldn't wear them. You're just saying they're not big enough to accommodate your manhood."

If looks could scorch, I'd be on fire. "Samantha, the only way I'll be inside your panties is if you're still wearing them."

Holy fuck.

I need a minute to recover from his smolder. I close my suitcase and zip it up. With a sigh, I face him. "I think that's it."

We get my suitcase downstairs, and I collect my backpack and purse from the library. When I come back to the front door, my mom is standing there in a daze between Joseph's parents. I drop my things on the floor and move to her, but she just stares at me. Actually, she's staring *through* me. There's no acknowledgment, no recognition in her eyes. Those once lively, full of love, pale green eyes are now glassy and blank. There is no emotion in them at all. No sadness. No anger. No nothing.

I wipe away my errant tear and touch her shoulder. "Mom, I'll see you soon." My voice cracks. Joseph is behind me before I even see him move. One hand grips my right side, the other squeezes my left hand, his front blanketing my back, protecting me, giving me strength to see this through. With steadier breath, I give Mom a quick unreturned hug, and step back.

Before I can sink into Joseph's arms, Fiona, Joseph's mom, embraces me. "She'll be alright. Give us a few days to get situated, and then let's chat about how she's doing."

I pull away and nod, returning to Joseph's side.

Not to be outdone, Hugh, Joseph's dad, pulls me into a warm bearhug. "If you need anything, I mean *anything*, you just call. Night or day." He pulls away, meeting his son's eyes. "Take care of her, Joseph."

I smile at the use of his full name.

"Of course." Joseph gives both his parents hugs. "We'll talk tomorrow."

As he closes the door behind them, he turns to me. "Give me a minute to double check the house is secure and then we'll go."

"I'll put my bags in my car." I pick up my purse and backpack.

"You won't need your car, and if you do need one, you can use one of mine or Fin's. Just give me five minutes, and I'll be ready."

He disappears up the stairs before I have a chance to even argue. And to be honest, I don't even want to. I'm sure I should, but at the moment, it feels good to be taken care of, including being driven around. He already shared that a car will drive me to and from school, which I'm good with. It means I get to do homework while on the road, or even just close my eyes and relax, have a moment of Zen.

Michael and his team follow us to Fin's. I wonder who else might be out there watching such a precession, or even joining without us knowing it.

PART 2
BEGINNING

Three

Joseph

S HE'S QUIET ON THE WAY TO FIN'S, UNTIL WE enter the parking garage at MCI Towers.

"Why do your brothers live here?"

"It's extremely convenient." I slip into one of Fin's parking spaces.

"Do they ever really get to leave work behind? Don't they end up working all hours of the night, just because they never leave their place of employment?" The censure is clear in her voice.

I stare at her, contemplating, before getting out of the car. I'm not sure if this really bothers her, or if she's trying to pick a fight in an effort to keep herself closed off from me. "I don't think Fin working long hours would change if he lived at another location. It would just mean he'd lose those productive hours commuting. Now, Matt's a whole other story. He works hard, but he plays hard too. If he didn't live so close to where he works, he probably wouldn't be as productive."

"Joseph, how can you not see that living where you work is not a good idea?"

I move around the car, drawing her close. "It works for them. Maybe not forever, but for now they're happy." I grab her bags out of the car and motion for her to follow.

Michael and his team have already swept the place and have men positioned in front of the elevators here in the garage and on the penthouse level where Fin and Matt live. Victor and his men are a little more discreet, monitoring the security cameras and their normal positions they cover for the MCI business as a whole. Having Samantha here will make it easier on Victor and his team, with cameras everywhere except in the penthouse itself.

I enter the elevator, situate the luggage, and only then realize I'm alone. She's stopped cold on the threshold of the elevator, not moving, just staring at me, lips pursed and brows furrowed.

"Is this where you plan to live when you graduate?" She seems bothered by the idea of it, and I'm not sure why.

I nod. "Probably—it's convenient and available." The doors start to close, and I quickly put my hand out to stop them. "Samantha, please." I motion for her to enter. We don't have time for this now. We need to get up to Fin's and get her settled, not stand here in the garage debating my family's living situation.

Surprisingly, she obeys my command and enters the elevator.

As we rise from the garage level, I slip the penthouse key into the control panel and enter the code granting us access to the top floor. Stepping back, I face her. "I never really thought much about not living here. I just assumed I would. There are four more penthouses in the other Omega Tower that are currently unoccupied. They're used for business occasionally, but my dad has left them empty so I'll have my pick if I choose to live here. My parents stay occasionally, if attending a late-night function downtown. There's security, twenty-four-hour concierge service, maid service, and a fleet of cars at our disposal. Let's talk in a couple of days and see if you still think the same about living here so close to MCI."

"It's only temporary for me. Additionally, I don't work here."

"You could live here. And you do work here, at least in the summers—for now," I say matter-of-factly.

The elevator chimes, announcing our arrival. I remove the key and step out before she can reply. Once I've got the luggage out of her way, she joins me in the marble vestibule with two large doors on opposite sides.

"This one is Fin's." Moving to the door on my left, I unlock it and motion over my shoulder. "The other door is Matt's."

I stand aside for her to enter, then set her bags down and close the door behind us. The light in the foyer is on but nothing else. Fin's at the office, having left Sam's before we did. He gave up most of his morning to help me with Samantha and her mom. It's a sacrifice and put a large dent in his agenda for the day.

"Lights," I command from behind her.

She jumps and scowls at me as if I gave her a direct order. Realization dawns as the entire place comes to life. Various lamps and recessed lighting turn on, some brighter than others, but a warm glow encompasses the entire living area. Then faint music fills the air. Samantha makes her way to the wall of windows in the living room.

"It's beautiful," she says almost reverently, taking in the downtown skyline of the city we both grew up in.

It is spectacular. I take a moment to enjoy the view. It's quite awe-inspiring to be in the middle of the skyline, a part of it. Up close and personal.

She turns and does a double take when she sees me smiling at her. "Still think it's so bad to live here?" I ask.

"I didn't say it was bad to live here. I just worry Fin never disconnects from work. Or maybe that's what he likes. It's a good excuse to be a workaholic."

"Hmmm. Let me show you to your room and give you the ten-cent tour."

I leave her to unpack and shower. I putter around in the kitchen, grabbing some grapes as I text with Fin to see what he wants to do for dinner. He quickly replies he has it covered and will be home around six. It's unusual for him to be home so early, but it's good for him to take a break now and again. Having Samantha here will be good. Give him something else, *someone* else to focus on.

Samantha is right—Fin is a workaholic, though I don't believe he's proud of that fact. I think it's just the way his life is right now. He takes on a lot, trying to take the strain away from our dad and our uncles. Dad is the oldest of his brothers, who all work for MCI in one aspect or another. Eventually, our cousins will come to work for MCI, if they choose to do so. It's always our preference to keep the company in the family; no one is going to care for it or understand its roots and its importance to our family as much as we do. My dad and his two brothers started at MCI just like my brothers did, and I will in a year's time.

My cousins are younger than me. I think the next-oldest one turns eighteen this year and starts college this fall. Therefore, it will be a few years before any other McIntyre heirs join the company full-time. Most start as young as we did, at thirteen, working in various departments over the summers, getting a feel for the business and finding their niche.

I look out over the skyline, looking forward to dusk when the city lights come to life. I never really doubted the idea of living at MCI Towers once I graduate college. It made sense to live here close to work, close to my brothers, who are also my friends. I'm trying to see it from Samantha's perspective and why she objects. It seems to be more than just the idea of being so close to work, and I need to find out what it is. Maybe not tonight, but before I make this my permanent residence. I need to dwell in the head of Samantha Cavanagh to see what exactly is bothering her and making her prickly to the idea of penthouse living.

Samantha

Incredible, I think as I turn off the shower. We're not poor by any means. My dad was a doctor and my mom an attorney, after all. We're upper middle class, I suppose. We live in a nice house with modern amenities, but never have I experienced a shower like this. Besides the fact it's big enough for six people, it has recessed adjustable rain shower heads across the top and more along the sides. There's even a control panel to adjust which heads are on, the temperature, and the desired spray type. I've never been so gloriously surrounded by water and not been submerged in it. It's calming, tranquil, and surprisingly sensual. I think I'm in love.

I reluctantly exit the shower, grabbing a towel from the warmer. *A warmer! Seriously.* Then head to the closet for some clothes. I search through the drawers trying to remember where I put everything when I quickly unpacked before jumping in the shower. I grab a t-shirt and yoga pants, matching bra and panties, and make my way back to the bathroom.

My shoulder wound is healing nicely. The hot shower helped loosen the muscles and reduce the constant ache. My doctor believes it should be healed enough to start physical therapy next week. I'm actually looking forward to it and hope I can say goodbye to the sling. I still wear it to school, and if my shoulder aches more than normal when at home.

With a sigh and a shake of my head, I give up the examination and move onto the business of drying my hair and getting dressed. When I'm done, I quietly slip out of my room and down the hall toward the living space. It's quiet. I'm not sure where Joseph even is.

Stopping at the entry, I scan the room. It really is a beautiful place and not too masculine, but definitely modern with a bit of old world rustic thrown in, which helps warm up the space with the marble floors and floor-to-ceiling windows.

My perusal of the space stops as soon as I spot Joseph, stretched out on the couch, sound asleep. I continue my path to the kitchen. A bottled water I find in the fridge will have to do as I don't want to wake him up with the ice dispenser. I pad back to the bedroom to get my tablet before making myself comfortable on the opposite couch.

Concentrating on my ebook seems pointless. I think I've read the same paragraph five times. My eyes keep wandering over to the sleeping man in front of me, his dark hair disheveled from his fingers, lying on his side, facing me. His arms are crossed over his chest, causing his muscles to bunch in such a way I just want to kiss, lick, suck, and possibly bite them. He looks peaceful, the emotions of this morning washed from his features by sleep.

It's hard to believe I met him for the first time four months ago. I, of course, knew of him via my internship with MCI, but I'd never met him or even seen him in person until Jace brought him home. Even in my fantasies, I never dreamed Joseph would want to be a part of my life, watching out for me, wanting to keep me safe despite the danger to his own life and that of his family. The truth is, though, if my dad hadn't died, Joseph would still be in Austin living his no-Samantha life. He would have kept his vow to not pursue a relationship. Not now, and maybe not ever.

But here we are, four months later having not been together, then been together, then not together again after I broke up with him two weeks ago. It's been turbulent at best and heartbreaking at worst. I don't trust it for so many reasons, but the bottom line is he's here because of my father's death, and that's not a reason that'll keep him with me for the long haul. It won't be a strong enough reason to overcome the obstacles we're still bound to face.

It doesn't mean I don't believe he cares for me. I believe he does. I'm not sure, though, if his feelings for me are stronger than his need to protect me. They may go hand in hand, or maybe his protective instincts are making him believe he feels more for me than he really does, clouding his vision of what his true feelings actually are. He's a caretaker by nature, a protector. I think if we were just friends, he would still feel the need to protect me, protect anyone he feels is in danger and he has the power to protect.

Obligation.

Maybe.

That's.

What.

I.

Am.

"Hey." Joseph's husky voice draws my eyes to his waking form. He frowns and sits up, rubbing his hands across his face. "What happened? Why are you crying, Sweetness?"

Shaking my thoughts away, I jump up, wiping my face. "Nothing. I'm fine." In the kitchen, I grab a bottled water and two glasses of ice.

In typical Joseph fashion, he doesn't let it drop easily. He doesn't let me hide. He takes the water and glasses out of my hands, setting them on the coffee table. "Come here, baby." He pulls me into his arms, over his lap, and back onto the couch as he lays us both down, facing each other. My head rests on his arm that circles around, pulling me closer as his other hand does the same on my lower back. He uses his leg to pull mine between his thighs. Once we're situated the way he wants, his attention turns back to me. He runs his hand tenderly across my cheeks, his gaze never veering from my face. "What is it?"

I shake my head. I can't tell him what I'm thinking. What I'm feeling. It will only upset him, and he'll say whatever he needs to say to convince me I'm wrong. But I'm not wrong. I burrow into the crook of his neck. "I don't want to talk. Just hold me. Please."

"Sweetness." He voice is gentle and kind like I'm the most precious thing to him.

But, I'm not. I can't be.

He pulls me tighter, our bodies pressed together, not a hair's breadth between us.

"Honey, I'm home," reaches into the depths of my sleep.

My head jerks up.

"Fin," Joseph growls. "Shhh. I got you, Samantha." He cups my face and kisses my brow. "I'm sorry he woke you up like that."

Still foggy from sleep, I bury my face in Joseph's chest, his warmth welcoming me back. "Hmmm."

His chest rumbles with laughter. "Just rest till dinner gets here."

I vaguely hear their conversation before drifting off to sleep again, lost in the comfort that exists only in his embrace. His chest. His smell. His possessiveness. His heart.

His.

Only.

His.

"Sweetness." His lips feather across mine.

I fight to remain in the world of the sleeping, and yet at the same time, fight to return to the man who's calling my name.

"Dinner's here. You need to wake up so I can feed you." His lips pass over mine again, just barely there.

"Feed her?" Fin scoffs.

Joseph stiffens as his arms squeeze me gently. "Asshole."

Warm lips press to mine.

One.

Two.

Three times.

Fin's laugh resonates from the distance. "Caveman."

I respond to his kiss before he can pull away or acknowledge his brother's comment, moving my hand to hold the back of his head, pressing him to me, ensuring our kiss continues. Lathing my tongue across the seam of his lips, he opens on a gasp, and I take full advantage, delving in deeper, holding him tighter, pressing against him and rolling my hips into him.

"Fuck, Samantha. You're gonna make me come if you keep kissing me like that," he whispers against my lips, sending chills down my spine.

To say the thrill roaring through my body at his admission of what I can do to him is no small thing, would be an understatement. It's everything.

"You say it like it's a bad thing," I tease, opening my eyes for the first time, taking in his emeralds that seem to burn just for me.

He chuckles and slaps my butt. "You need to get up so we can eat."

"Killjoy," I grumble as I extricate myself from his body, standing up slowly to stretch and catch my bearings.

Fin smirks at me from the kitchen. "Good evening, Sam."

I can't help the sleepy smile and small laugh at his greeting. "Good evening, Fin." I enter the kitchen. "How was work?"

He pulls down plates from the cabinet, and I take them from him, silently asking where to place them. He motions to the dining room as he grabs flatware and tells me about his day, or at least the part of his day I'm not already privy to since he was with us for much of it.

I set down three plates but notice there's a fourth one. "Who else is joining us?"

His Cheshire Cat smile is beyond devious. "I invited a friend to dinner. I thought you might enjoy the company and even out the ratio a bit."

"The ratio?" I glance to Joseph, who shakes his head.

"Yes, the male-to-female ratio," Fin says matter-of-factly, handing me the utensils and napkins before returning to the kitchen.

I grin, catching Joseph's eye. "Fin invited a girl over. A female friend." I cock my head around the corner. "I didn't think you had any female friends, Fin."

"Sam, you don't know me well enough to make that assessment," he says simply. No animosity, just a point of fact.

"Yep, I guess you're right." I shrug and finish setting the table.

A few moments later, the doorbell rings. Fin stops what he's doing in the kitchen and disappears around the corner with that damn Cheshire smile still on his face.

Four

Joseph

DINNER IS GOOD, BUT THE COMPANY IS BETTER. Particularly the company of my girl. She kissed the hell out of me earlier, topping off the joy of holding her in my arms as she napped. I don't know what upset her, and I hope to find out later, but at the moment I'm happy to watch her laugh and banter back and forth between the four of us as if we do this all the time. It's easy. Natural. The way it's meant to be. The way I imagine it always could be.

The surprise guest is Margot, Samantha's good friend. I suspect Samantha refuses to call Margot her best friend out of respect for Jace. I would say Jace lost that slot a long time ago, though I'm not sure he truly ever earned that title in the first place. However, that's not my call to make. I'm still angry at him about Tiff. I'm definitely not the best judge of his character or his worthiness to be called Samantha's best friend.

"What do you mean you don't go in the water?" Fin reacts to Margot's dismissal of his invite to join us at the lake house this summer.

She stares at Samantha as she answers, her eyes pleading. There's a story behind that look.

"Well, I don't wear swimsuits, so I don't go in the water." Margot offers as explanation, but it actually raises more questions than answers.

"Ever?" Fin's shock is apparent on his face and in the volume of his response.

I stifle a laugh. He's getting all worked up as if it's the most ridiculous thing he's ever heard.

Samantha pokes at her food, moving it around her plate. She puts down her fork, giving Margot a quick smile. "She's sensitive to sunlight, so it doesn't make much sense to hang out at the lake or the pool."

"But do you swim?" Fin questions further.

"Uh…yes." Margot shimmies uncomfortably in her chair.

I can't figure out what's really going on here between Fin's interest in this topic and Margot in general, and Margot and Samantha's evasiveness, but I'm quite intrigued myself. I also find it funny he hasn't caught on that she obviously doesn't want to talk about it, but Fin just keeps digging.

"Do you go to the lake often?" Samantha directs the question to Fin and me.

Fin responds quickly, barely giving his brain time to process the question. "I think we could stand to go more often, particularly if you two joined us."

I think Fin really likes Margot. I gave him crap about it when we ran into her and her sister in Austin, but in typical Fin fashion he brushed it off, making light of his suspected interest in her. The fact he wanted me to invite her for dinner doesn't bode well for his supposed disinterest in her.

"Sam, we thought you and Margot might like to take a spa day tomorrow." Fin drops the surprise we've been hatching.

I take Samantha's hand. "You're off the rest of the week, and it's been arranged for Margot to go with you tomorrow if you're up for it. We thought you could use a day of pampering and relaxation." One day is not going to erase the stress of the last month since her father died, but it's a start. I want her to use these next few days to just relax and recharge, not worrying about being in control of anything. She needs to step back and just worry about herself for a while.

Samantha's wide eyes roam the three of us before landing back on me. "Seriously?" The smile gracing her face is precious. I want to do whatever I can to put that look on her face as often as possible.

I squeeze her hand. "Yes, Sweetness. Anything you want, for as long as you want."

She claps her hands, bouncing in her seat, and asks Margot, "You knew about this?"

Margot's smile matches Samantha's, and for a moment I'm not sure who's more excited about this spa day. "Yes! I was dying to tell you, but promised to keep my mouth shut until the menfolk broke the surprise." She rolls her eyes, glancing between Fin and me.

"Victor will be here at ten to pick you up, and Margot will meet you there," Fin fills her in on the details.

Samantha bounds out of her chair and gives Fin a kiss on the cheek. "Thank you, Fin. Truly. Thank you."

She then bounces over to me and kisses me on the lips. "And thanks to you, too."

"You're welcome, Sweetness."

Samantha captures Margot in a hug. "I'm so excited. This will be so fun."

The two of them get lost in conversation about tomorrow as Fin and I begin to clean up dinner.

Samantha

Margot left right after dinner, but not before I pulled her aside to apologize for lying to her about my birthday plans. She doesn't really understand, but she forgives me and knows she probably wouldn't have left it alone if I had told her I just wanted to be by myself. Just as Jace or Joseph wouldn't let it slide either. They think they want me to be upfront with them, but in truth, none of them wants to hear how much I didn't want to celebrate.

"Sam." Fin catches me as I close the door behind Margot and hands me an envelope. "Here's a key to the penthouse and the elevator, the code for the elevator, the code for the alarm system, and cardkey for the garage."

"Wow. That's a lot of information." My head spins trying to process the importance of what's inside this flat white envelope.

"You don't need to worry about any of that for tomorrow, but I want you to have it, just in case. Victor will see to it when you leave for the spa and when you come back. I'll show you how to use it all after I get home."

"Thank you, Fin. For everything." I surprise him with a hug, but it doesn't take him long to hug me back.

"You're welcome." He kisses my head before releasing me. "I'm glad you're taking a day to relax and recharge. No one could have handled what you've had to endure with more grace and dignity. You're not alone anymore. I'm here. Joseph is here, even though he won't always be here physically. Matt and my parents all want to help, as well as Michael and Victor."

I nod, not trusting my voice. I don't understand the level of commitment his family is showing me, but I appreciate it and am touched by it all the same.

I join Joseph and Fin in the living room, listening to them discuss work. Normally, I'm endlessly fascinated with the world of MCI, but it's making me uncomfortable tonight. The idea of Joseph living in a penthouse like this in a year's time drills home the point that they live in a different world than I'm accustomed to. I'm the worker-bee, not the queen. Joseph needs a queen. I know we discussed it before, but this just brings it all crashing back, reality shining brighter than the lights outside Fin's penthouse window, a beacon of the life that awaits Joseph. A high-end, fancy, busy life as a MCI VP.

Add on my doubts over his feelings being heightened as the result of my father's death, the fact he slept with someone else, and that I'm putting them all in danger by simply being here—my anxiety boils over. I hop up with the excuse of getting a drink.

Out of their sight, I pace the kitchen, trying to contain my emotions and raging thoughts. I drink two glasses of water before I decide what I need to do.

Both men stop talking as I reenter the living room. Joseph frowns when he sees me, reading me all too easily.

"I'm going to go to my room." It's only eight, so I can't really say I'm going to bed. "Uh…Fin, thank you for letting me stay. I guess I'll see you tomorrow night."

"Goodnight, Sam. Please call me tomorrow if you need anything." He watches me warily as if he can read me too.

Joseph's eyes narrow, his muscles flex, ready to pounce.

He knows.

I clear my throat, trying to gain strength. "I guess I'll see you… sometime? Thank you for everything. Goodnight."

He stands. "Samantha." His voice is pained with the reality of what I'm trying to do.

I hold my hand up, as if the motion alone would calm him and release him of his self-imposed responsibilities. "Just…don't. Let me go, Joe. It's better this way."

"Goddammit, Samantha!" He stalks across the room too quickly for me to react beyond a few bumbled words and a graceless step backward.

I yelp as he lifts me off my feet and throws me over his shoulder. "I told you." He grips my legs, holding me secure. "I warned you."

"Put me down! You can't do this!" I protest and slap his ass.

"Sweetness," he says all too calmly, "we discussed this. I told you what would happen if you called me that name again. I'm nothing if not a man of my word."

"You can't do this!" I reiterate, holding on to his hips. "Fin, tell him he can't do this."

"Joe." Fin arches a brow at his brother. Their silent exchange happens in a blink of an eye. "Sam." He addresses me now. "Do you really want me to interfere?"

Do I? He would. I can see it in his eyes. Do I want or need Fin in the middle of what's going on with Joseph and me? Isn't it complicated enough without me dragging Fin in to play referee?

Besides, I *don't* want him to stop this. I want Joseph to fight for me. Not out of obligation. Not out of misplaced feelings. I need him to want me for me, as I am now, and not who I may or may not be in the future. "No," I say softly.

Fin nods. "Fair enough."

Joseph grunts and heads toward the hall leading to my room.

"Joe." Fin's voice stops him in his tracks. "Remember who she is—who she is to *you*."

Joseph lets out a huff of air. "I know exactly *who* she is—*what* she is to me," he barks back, turning and continuing on his path. "*She's* the one who needs reminding, and that's what I intend to do."

Holy shit!

Five

Joseph

TO SAY I'M ANGRY WOULD NOT FULLY encapsulate the depth of what I'm currently feeling. I'm angry as hell and frustrated. I'm hurt by her need to pull away from me—despite the danger she'd willingly put herself in to do it—and pained knowing I'm partially to blame. I'm roaring with possessiveness and the need to mark my territory by sinking my cock balls deep into her to prove she's *mine*.

But fuck. I can't treat her like that. She deserves better. Always.

I plunk her down on the bed, placing my hand on her chest, my thumb and fingers bracketing the space between her collarbones. "Don't move." I hold her down, gently. I'm too angry. *Fuck.* "I need a minute." To calm the fuck down. I start to remove my hand, but she tries to sit up.

I push her back down. "Christ, Samantha. Fucking listen to me for once!"

She lies back, surprised by my vehemence. I brush my free hand across my face. "I won't hurt you. I swear, I could never hurt you, Sweetness. But you're pushing me away—don't deny it—and I need a minute to calm down." I stand up, moving away from the bed. "Give me that, please."

She nods. Her eyes soften as she watches me. "Okay."

I let out a long breath and move to the other end of the room. The curtains are open. Night has come alive outside her bedroom windows.

It's nearly as beautiful as she is, though it can't truly hold a candle to her incandescence. Just the thought of that starts to calm me. I glance over at her. She's in the same spot, focusing on me.

I come back to her, grabbing my t-shirt at the back of my neck and pulling it off over my head. Her eyes widen as she takes in my bare chest. My cock swells to painful proportions. I'm not naked enough.

I stop at the edge of the bed. "Take your top off, Sweetness." Silently, she shifts to pull her t-shirt off, taking extra time in extricating her right arm, revealing a pale purple bra cupping her breast provocatively. Her breathing increases, and her chest moves up and down to accommodate her increased heart rate's need for more air.

"Fuck, you're beautiful," I whisper.

I quickly discard my pants and boxer briefs, and crawl up her body, stopping only to kiss up her exposed abdomen and sides.

"Joseph," she breathes.

Thank fuck. She remembers my name.

"That's right, baby. Say it again and again until you know me by no other name." I run my lips across the silken cups of her bra as my fingers trace the lace edges along the top curve of each billowing breast. "I can feel your nipples." I run my lips across each hidden peak again, baring my teeth to scrape the ridged swells. "They're hard for me, Samantha. Just like my cock is hard for you."

Her hands clasp my shoulders as she arches toward my mouth, gasping.

"Yes, baby. So fucking beautiful." I reach underneath her and unclasp her bra with one quick twist. Sitting back, I slowly trail the sexy yet inhibiting bra off her glorious tits. Her eyes blaze with heat when I bend down and flick my tongue over one taut nipple.

"Joseph."

I can't help but smile. "That's right. Say it again." I flick my tongue over her other stiff peak.

She remains silent, yet her hand laces into my hair, trying to draw me to her.

I resist. "What's my name, Sweetness?" I flick her nipple again. "What's my name to *you*?"

"Joseph," she moans.

"Yes. Again." I draw her nipple into my mouth, and this time she chants my name as I suck, pull, and bite on her luscious offerings. I don't give her any respite as I take her other one in my mouth, my fingers continue to tease, pinch, twist her wet and swollen peak I just abandoned. I continue back and forth, torturing her, loving her, making her mine in every way I can until I can make her mine in the most intimate of ways.

Her head tips back, begging me for more, my name escaping her lips over and over again with abandon.

My cock bobs against her belly, anxious to claim her, and my need to touch her roars through my body. *Make her come.*

I slip my hand into her yoga pants and inside her panties. When I touch her slick flesh, she bows off the bed.

"Yes. Please," she pleads.

I place her hand on my cock. "Touch me, Sweetness. I need you too."

Her moan as she touches me for the first time nearly has me coming like a first-time teenager. "Fuck, just like that. Squeeze and pull it, baby."

I slip between her folds, wetting my fingers and moving back to her swollen clit. "We're gonna come together."

She squeezes my cock as her thumb rubs my pre-cum around my cock head.

"And then I'm going to lick you and taste you until you're so hoarse, you can't cry my name any longer, but you'll still be saying it in your head as I drink you up."

She clenches, and her whole body trembles. "Joseph, I'm gonna come."

I press harder and watch as she detonates under me. Her skin flushes, mouth open, crying out my name as her body rocks against my fingers.

Her cries of ecstasy and her hand on my cock take me with her. "Fuck, yes. Just like that." I pump into her hand as I mark her with my cum, feeling all too proud to be doing so, and still hard as fuck.

"Joseph." She continues to grind against my fingers. I don't stop.

I suck her nipples and stroke her clit into two more orgasms. I come again on the third one. Her hand never left my cock. Her hunger for me is just as strong as mine for her.

—♡—

Samantha

Joseph kisses me awake a little after midnight. "I have to go, Sweetness."

"What?" I try to sit up to focus on what he's saying, but he keeps me still, his body over mine. He's no longer naked, and I'm disappointed. "You're dressed?"

He smiles at my surprise. "Yes. They tend to frown when you arrive at the tarmac naked. I think it's some kind of FAA regulation or something," he teases.

"I don't want anyone else to see you naked." I'm not teasing. The whole jealousy thing is back, and I'm instantly inundated with thoughts of the girl he fucked a few weeks ago. Tears prick my eyes. "Why do you have to leave? I thought you were going to stay since it's just one more day of school for you. You don't have class on Fridays."

"You're right. I don't have school on Fridays, but I need to be back for class today."

"Oh." I can't hide my disappointment.

He kisses my head and then moves to sit next to me, pulling my naked body into his lap. "I need to give you your birthday present."

His sheepish smile is almost enough to chase the sadness away. "You got me a present?"

"Yes. I've had it for a while, but I wanted to wait and give it to you on your birthday."

"How long have you had it?" I'm looking around and don't see any presents laying on the bed.

"I got it over Christmas before I mauled you on your date with Sebastian."

"That wasn't a date," I correct.

"It wasn't a date for *you*. It was a date for him until he and I came to an understanding," he clarifies.

"Hmm. Well, if that's a mauling, then you can maul me like that anytime." I squirm at the memory of the way Joseph stormed the restaurant and made me come in an alcove where we could have been discovered, claiming me like I was his.

He grips my hips to still me. "You're going to make me hard if you keep that up."

I move to straddle him, his growing erection pressing between my legs. I lean forward and whisper in his ear, "Too late." I kiss his neck and suck his earlobe. "I want to taste you."

His hands grab my hips again. "Christ, Samantha." He's turned on and wants it too. But still he denies me. "I didn't make good on my promise to kiss and lick every inch of you. We'll have to save that for next time."

I start to move away. But he stops me, holding me tightly against him. "Where you going?"

"You said *no*," I say softly, keeping my eyes on his clothed chest.

He lifts my chin with a finger. "I said no to a taste test. I'm not saying no to letting you get me off again." He kisses my chin and then my lips, tenderly, before pulling way. "I don't think I could ever deny you wanting to touch me."

I see the truth in his eyes.

He motions to the bed. "Lie down."

I quickly comply as Joseph stands, stripping off his clothes. He throws the covers to the end of the bed and turns the nightstand lamp on before he lies beside me.

"I want to see you. I need to remember this moment for when I'm away from you." His eyes roam my body and settle on my face. "You're the most beautiful creature I've ever seen." He leans down and kisses my neck and then moves lower to my nipples, hard in anticipation of his touch. "Spread your legs for me. Show me that glorious pussy."

"Joseph," I gasp, loving his dirty talk but shocked by it too.

He smiles wickedly as he sucks my nipple into his mouth and moves his hard cock against my thigh.

I arch and spread my legs for him, wanting him in ways I don't understand in places I've never been touched before.

He groans as I take his hand and press it between my thighs. "Christ, that's hot." He watches as his fingers slip through my wet slit. "Show me what you need."

I move my hips against his fingers, wanting him to enter me, but he doesn't. I wrap my hand around his cock and tease his moist head before moving up and down his shaft in time with my hips.

"So fucking beautiful, Sweetness." His eyes never leave mine as our bodies soar once again.

He growls at the clock. "I'm late."

Finishing getting dressed, he comes back to sit next to me on the bed. His hand slips below the covers to between my legs. "I can't get enough of this, Samantha." He pulls back, slipping his fingers into his mouth with a groan.

OMG! That's so hot.

"Next time, I'm spending all night with you coming on my tongue and face."

How can I be turned on again? My hips move of their own accord. My hand rubs his jean-clad erection. He closes his eyes and moves his hips into my hand as his fingers slip below the covers again. "Show me." His voice is low with need.

I pull back the covers and spread my legs, no longer shy of showing him what he does to me.

"You want me, Sweetness?" One-handed, he undoes his jeans,

pulling out his rigid cock, wrapping his fingers around it, stroking it hard and fast.

The sight of him pleasuring himself is nearly too much. "Yes." I arch back, needing more.

He fingers move lower, rounding my entrance, teasing but not entering me. "You want me here? You want my cock filling you up?"

"God, yes."

He moans at my eagerness. "Touch your breast for me. Make your nipples hard. Make it feel good."

I grab each breast and squeeze. My nipples harden under my palms. I pull and twist slightly, sending currents of pleasure to my clitoris.

"Slip your fingers inside your pussy, baby. Fuck yourself for me. Let me watch." He's so turned on, cum beads on the head of his cock.

I reach over and swipe it, licking it off my fingers, before lowering my hand between my legs.

"Fuck, Samantha," he groans as I slip my fingers into my virgin passage. "That right there is the hottest damn thing I've ever seen."

He continues to circle my clit with one hand as he strokes his cock with the other, watching my fingers slip in and out. "Fuck, you need to get there. I'm about to come just from the sight of you."

I can't keep my eyes off his near-bursting cock. I want to run my tongue along the tip, licking the cum as it escapes.

"Curl your fingers, baby, just a few inches in and press." His gravelly voice nearly sends me over.

I do it. A whole new sensation causes me to clench around my fingers. "Oh, god!"

"That's your g-spot, beautiful. Stroke it." He watches my fingers slip in and out. "That's right, just like that. Tell me. What does it make you want?"

"You. You inside me, filling me, rubbing me right there with the head of your cock. And yet I need you deeper too."

My words hit me more than they do him. I'm overcome. "Joseph." I close my eyes and twist my head away. It's too much.

Suddenly, he's over me. His mouth is on one nipple as his hand teases the other one. I open my eyes, and he's no longer touching himself. He's totally focused on me.

"What about you?" I grab his cock and stroke him in rhythm with my fingers. Fuck, that's erotic. I can feel it, the tingling starting in my legs.

He grunts against my breast and sucks harder, biting down slightly. That does it. The most powerful orgasm I've ever felt rips through my body. I grip him tighter, trying not to forget him as I shake and clench around my fingers, coming for his pleasure and mine.

Minutes, possibly hours later, I open my eyes to Joseph sitting next to me sucking on my fingers and wiping off my abdomen and then between my legs with a warm washcloth.

Panic hits me. "Oh, god, did you come?" I don't even remember if I let go of him or if he even came. I was too wrapped up in my own release to focus on him.

He releases my fingers with a *pop*. "All over you, Sweetness." His dimpled smile is stunning.

Taking the washrag back to the bathroom, he returns a moment later, beaming, relaxed, and satisfied. He lies next to me, fully dressed, and pulls me into his arms. "That was the hottest sexual experience of my life. I've never been so turned on or come so hard." He kisses my forehead. "Actually, I've never come that many times in one night. Ever."

I shyly nuzzle into his neck, entirely too sated and happy to even respond except to say, "Me neither. But, I suppose you already knew that."

He lifts my chin. "I could spend hours talking to you about that, but I have something important I have to do before I leave. And I really have to leave or I'll never get back to Austin."

Reaching into his pocket, he pulls something out. "This is a sign of my devotion to you. It represents my promise to you of a future I'm determined we'll have together."

He slips a ring on my left ring finger, and brings my hand to his lips and kisses it. "Forever, Samantha. This is my promise."

"Joseph—" I start to protest.

He stops me with a kiss, deepening it more than he should if he intends to leave. He pulls back, breathless, just like me. "You need time. You need to process what all has happened. Not just tonight, but over the last few weeks. I hurt you. I slept with someone else. Intentional or not, it still happened, and you need time to process that."

Intentional or not?

He squeezes my hand. "I need you to forgive me. I need you to come to trust what you are to me, and what I am to you. Not just now but in the future. Our future. Together." Kissing me one more time, he slips out of bed, tucking me in. "I'll talk to you tomorrow." Then he smiles. "Well, later today actually. I set your alarm for nine in the morning. Victor will pick you up at ten for your spa day. Take your phone and your ear buds. I'm going to send you something, and you'll need them."

I start to panic, and tears cloud my vision. "Joseph." I grip his arms tightly, not wanting to let him go. When he's here and close, all feels right. It's when he's gone, away from me, I start to crumble and begin to question everything.

As if he can read my mind, he takes both my hands in his and holds up my left hand so I can see the platinum band of solid diamonds he's placed on my finger. "Do you see this ring?" He waits for me to nod before he continues. "This ring is my promise to you, my commitment to you and our future. When you have doubts, when you're scared, lonely, or mad at me, just look down at your finger and know I'm here."

He kisses the ring, my palm, and each finger, then presses my ring-clad hand over his heart. "And know you are here. Always. Promise."

PART 3
FALLING

Six

Samantha

A T EXACTLY TEN THERE'S A KNOCK ON THE penthouse door. I look through the peephole, although whoever it is needs a key in order to make it up to this floor unannounced. There's a wall of chest staring back at me. I slowly open the door, not 100% sure it's such a good idea.

"Good morning, Sam." He gives me a quick nod, his face stoic, not giving up any thoughts dancing around in his head. *Dancing* may be a little too lighthearted for this man. His thoughts probably *stomp* around in his head.

"Morning, Victor." I give him a warm smile trying to coax one in return.

"Are you ready for your spa appointment?"

"Yep."

Victor sets the alarm, and then escorts me out the door and to the elevator.

He's a striking man, late twenties and built like a linebacker, probably about the same height as Joseph.

Yes, I will probably forever compare all men to Joseph. He's my new standard of measurement, apparently.

Victor has blond hair, a square jaw, and a neck the size of my thigh. He has light brown eyes and a hard-set mouth. He's so serious, his face might actually crack if he did smile. He's wearing a black suit that has to be custom made to fit such a muscular guy.

"Victor, you're not really a driver, are you?" He's way too fit; he has to be a bodyguard, at the least. I don't know his background, but he's an ex-military type, perfect for running security.

When I met him at the hospital, Fin introduced him as his long-time friend and driver. I thought it was kinda odd, but I guess a busy man like Fin needs to be able to concentrate on other tasks while driving around the city. I wonder which came first, the friend or the driver part, but just yesterday Joseph told me *Victor and his men* have been watching me for weeks. So obviously, he's not really a driver.

"Well, Sam, I'm driving you today. So, technically I am a driver."

Smartass.

I glare at him, unblinking, cock my head, my hand on my hip, trying to stare him to death until he admits he's more than just a driver.

I almost get a smirk. "That laser-beam glare of yours won't even penetrate my thick skin. You might as well give it up before you pop a blood vessel." He has a slight Texas drawl and a steely façade I'm determined to crack.

I sigh and look away. "Fine. If you won't tell me, then I'll just have to make up my own back story and job duties for you." The elevator doors open, I step out. "You may not like some of them. Fair warning."

"Duly noted." He motions to the left. "This way."

Did I detect a hint of amusement in his voice? Am I getting to him already? *Hmmm, this might be fun.*

The ride to the spa is quiet and peaceful. Margot is meeting us there, so I'm enjoying these few minutes of solitude. Not that Margot's a chatterbox, but when we get together, we are usually anything but quiet. We've been fairly good friends since second grade, but became closer when Jace went off to college. Jace still holds the title of "best friend," and it's hard to let go. It feels like I'm betraying him if I do, but honestly, I'm not sure he'd even notice with how distant he's been lately.

While I've always considered Jace my best friend, I've never really shared everything with him. I realized this past Thanksgiving, perhaps I don't really have a best friend. The situation at the dance club, where

I told Joseph my history with Jace's old hookup Veronica, made me realize I don't really tell anyone anything—not important things. I never told a soul about the shitty way Veronica treated me by seducing my then *kinda* boyfriend. Until I told Joseph, only Veronica and Roger knew what they did to me.

And while it wasn't technically cheating because Joseph and I were already broken up when he slept with someone else, part of me still feels like I've been cheated on again. I pushed him away to keep him safe, and the worst thing happened, so why am I letting him back in?

It could all go horribly wrong *again.*

Am I selfish enough to let them in and put them in danger? Or do I continue to keep everyone at arm's length and hope my father's killer focuses on me, ignoring everyone else?

"You alright, Sam?"

I meet Victor's eyes in the rearview mirror. "Yeah, why?"

He seems worried. Silently, he hands me a tissue. It's only then I realize I'm crying.

Shit. What is wrong with me? I've got to get a grip. I wipe my face. "I'm sorry. It's been one of those kinds of weeks."

"No need to apologize. You've had more than just a rough week." The concern is evident in his voice.

"Yeah. I guess you know all my dirty laundry." I lay my head back and close my eyes.

"Sam, we're here." I jump, but Victor stops me with a soft grip. "I didn't mean to scare you. I tried to be gentle." He's apologetic, like being gentle is foreign to him.

I nod and take a deep breath. "It's okay." I rub my head, trying to soothe the dull ache.

"Do you have a headache?" He's not the hard ass he wants me to think he is.

"No." I stare past him to the glass doors in front of me.

"Ms. Dubois is already here. Once you check in, they'll bring you to her." For a moment, I think he's talking about Margot's mother, but I realize he's referring to Margot. She'll get a kick out of being called Ms. Dubois.

My gaze moves back to the hulk of a man leaning down next to me in the open car door. "How long do we have? How do I get in touch with you?"

"I'm at your disposal, Sam. If you stay for an hour, or if you stay for six, it is completely up to you. Though, Ms. Dubois' parents ask she be home by eight, given it's a school night, and she's already playing hooky with you today." There— almost a hint of a smile.

"I can't imagine staying here that long. Maybe a massage and a pedicure, a few hours, tops."

I move to get out. Victor stands, offering me his hand in assistance.

"Give me your phone. I'll put my number in. You can call me or text when you're ready." I pull it out of my purse and hand it to him.

As I wait, I stretch my sore shoulder and try not to fidget.

He hands me back my phone, eyeing my bad shoulder for a moment. "No rush, no advance notice needed."

With a nod I head to the door.

"Sam." He moves closer, standing in my space so that I have to crane my neck to make eye contact.

"I do more than drive for Mr. McIntyre." He nods curtly and backs off, seemingly satisfied, as if he's relinquished a huge secret.

I study him for a beat. "No dice, Mary Poppins, that in no way equals the crap you know about me." I head toward the door. "The stakes have changed. Enjoy washing Fin's unmentionables."

I disappear inside. It takes everything I have not to turn around to see if any reaction shows on his face. Though, not knowing doesn't stop a huge smile from spreading across mine.

Game on, Victor.

After ditching my clothes and purse, I don a sumptuous white robe that's two sizes too big, but honestly, it feels amazing, and the large size is like wearing a blanket of the highest quality. It feels good against my bare skin. Decadent even. I find Margot sitting in a private lounge, relaxing on a caramel-colored chaise, reading a book. She's old school, preferring hardcopy as opposed to my ebook preference.

I take the lounger next to hers. She's lost in her book and has no idea I've even entered the room.

"I'm pretending to be sophisticated," she says quietly, her eyes focused on the page.

Well, so much for thinking I'm stealthy. "And what makes you think you have to pretend?"

Her eyes meet mine. "You and I both know that's not true." She shakes her head and smiles. "This place is supercalifragilisticexpialidocious, and I'm trying to contain my girlish desire to dance around in excitement." She straightens her shoulders and raises her chin. "Sophisticated, see?"

I study her, then nod succinctly. "Yes, I can see that. Very sophisticated indeed."

She beams, playing along, but then her face falls. "I have to ask. Don't be mad."

"You can ask me anything. I won't get mad."

She closes her book, setting it to rest beside her. "Did she ever remember?"

I stifle a flinch when I catch her train of thought. I'd wanted to spend it alone, but I can't deny the fact my own mother forgot my birthday stings like hell, despite the circumstances. That's how I know she's truly lost right now. My mom—and my dad—were amazing parents. But as amazing as they were, they were even more amazing as a couple. Awe-inspiring and everything I ever want in a mate. What my mom lost when he died was more than a partner—he was her soulmate, and I can't be mad at her or even disappointed in her. If celebrating my birthday can't bring her back, I don't know what it's going to take. "No," I sigh.

"It makes me sad to think about you being alone and Eleanor forgetting it was even your special day. She always makes such a fuss over birthdays. She even makes a fuss over *my* birthday." She's nearly in tears.

Sweet Margot, genuinely sad and offended for me.

I can't have that. I already cried once this morning, and even though we're not together, maybe Mom will snap out of it while with Joseph's parents. *That* is more important than any birthday present or fuss that could have been made. "That's why it's no big deal. If my father were still alive, it would've been a completely different day. But, the reality is—it's a new reality. My mom may never be the birthday-celebrating Eleanor again. She might be a whole different Eleanor, in every way."

Margot leans over and squeezes my hand. "I'm sorry."

I smile a smile I'm not feeling, but I'll fake it until I do. "Me too."

She swings her legs over the side to face me. "So, what are we having done today? Did you decide on a treatment?"

"Yes." I pick up the menu on the end table and point to the massage with a name I can't pronounce, so I don't even try. "I want this one. It's an-hour-and-a-half and sounds incredibly relaxing. Then I want the pedicure with the paraffin wax treatment."

"That's the massage I asked for too. Great minds think alike. I could go for a pedicure. That sounds like an excellent plan." She points to a button on the wall. "They said just ring the bell when we're ready."

I push the button, and almost immediately, two women come to get us. Before we separate, Margot gives me quick hug. "Thank you for including me. I'll see you afterwards for lunch."

Samantha

The massage was everything I hoped for. It was a little awkward at first, me being naked and all. I mean, she's a professional, but still, it's the idea of being naked with a stranger's hands on me.

She went to town on my shoulders, taking special care with my injured one. She kept telling me I carry my stress in my shoulders and neck, and that I'm far too young to have as much stress as she was working out of my body.

Hello? I've been shot. I've lost my father. Killer on the loose. And my on-again off-again piece of man-cake drama is enough to put me over the edge. Stress in my shoulders is minor collateral damage.

After the full body massage, she cocooned me in a therapeutic wrap and started a warm oil drip on my forehead. The scent of eucalyptus, lavender, and vanilla wafted in the air. I actually dozed off when she began to massage the oil into my scalp.

I stir when she starts to remove the warm blankets and the cool air hits my warmed, sensitized skin.

"I'm sorry to wake you, Ms. Cavanagh." Her smile is sweet and comforting. "You looked so peaceful, it's a shame."

I stifle a yawn. "It's okay." I scan the room, wondering how much time has passed. "I'm so relaxed. Thank you, that was wonderful."

She slips a dry sheet over me before removing the last of the damp towels from underneath the sheet. "I'm glad you enjoyed it. Now, be sure to drink plenty of water. You'll need to flush out all those toxins I released from your muscles."

With my promise to do just that, and a final thank you, she slips out of the room to leave me to shower.

I'm feeling weak and a little overheated, so a hot shower is not in the cards. I stay in just long enough to shampoo the oil out of my hair. With a quick blow dry and a slathering of the wonderful smelling lotion she left as a sample, I slip my robe back on and go in search of Margot.

The spa set up a private lunch in the same lounge we were in before. Margot isn't there when I enter, so I take a seat on a lounge chair and pull out my phone. My heart flutters when I see a text from Joseph.

Joseph: *Sweetness. I hope you're enjoying your spa day. Listen to this and know I'm thinking of you. (I will deny it if you tell anyone I've even ever heard of One Direction).*

I put in my earbuds and click the link in his text. My YouTube app opens and the video of "Little Things" by One Direction starts to play.

I've never been much of a One Direction fan, but I may start to love them as I listen to the song Joseph wanted me to hear, telling me he loves all these little things about me...and that he loves me.

Seriously? Did he just tell me he loves me through this song?

Self-consciously, I glance around the room, confirming I'm still alone. I hit play again and dash away the tears as they fall. No matter how hard I've fought it, I can't help falling in love with this man. I know it's too soon, and I'm struggling with the conflict of letting him go to keep him safe and keeping him close because I need him. I let my emotions run free until the end. Then, I search for the perfect song to send back in retribution.

I laugh out loud when I find it. It's scandalous, and he might not find any humor in it, but I need to stop this sentimental love train before it sweeps me away.

Me: *I promise to keep your One D obsession to myself. Here's a song for your listening pleasure. Enjoy.*

I include the link to the "Birthday Cake" by Rihanna video. It is definitely not One D. It's hot and sexy and gives a completely different idea of what I want. It's not that I don't want the hearts and flowers, I do. I truly do. I just don't want to get wrapped up in believing in the fairytale of Joseph and me. Not yet. It's too soon. I'm in danger, which means if he stays near me, *he'll* be in danger.

And he slept with someone else two weeks ago.

It's too fucking soon.

Plus, I'm not convinced he doesn't deserve better than me. I will be heartbroken when he finally figures that out. So, I'll send him sex songs to combat his romantic love songs.

That way, when he comes to his senses and realizes he's more protective over me than in love with me, maybe it will be easier because I haven't bought into the delusion from the start. Until then, until it all blows over, it's best if we—if I—keep things casual.

A good defense is a good offense—or so they say.

Margot and I have a salad of roasted chicken, candied walnuts, carrots, red onion, blue cheese, and heirloom tomatoes with a sweet vinaigrette that knocks my taste buds for a loop.

Maybe not all that healthy, but it was darn tasty.

"Holy nut crackers, Sam. What's on your finger?" She drops her fork and grabs my hand before I can pull it away. "Did he propose? Are you engaged?" Her voice gets louder with each word and is nearly a shrill by the time she reaches *engaged.*

"No. Calm down." I snatch my hand back, checking the room. Thankfully we're still alone, which seems odd. I wonder if it's by design.

Shit. It is.

I can't believe I didn't see it before. Joseph or Fin or fucking Michael made sure we would be alone, undisturbed, safe. I sink back into my chair and take in how that makes me feel. Cherished. Protected. Loved.

"Sam." Margot's worried voice pulls my attention.

"I'm sorry. I just realized we haven't seen another customer. They must have arranged it."

She takes in the room. It's clearly meant to be a community gathering place to wait or relax between treatments. Granted it's during the week, but still, the people who can afford to come here wouldn't be concerned about working hours as most of the women probably don't even work. Not that being the wife of a highly successful man is not work, it's just not nine-to-five work.

Margot's knowing gaze returns to mine. "You're right. I didn't think about it, but it seems so obvious now. Wow." She leans back, her awe mirroring mine. "He must really love you to go to all this trouble and cost."

"It might not even be Joseph who did this. It was probably Fin or Michael."

She shakes her head. "No. Uh-uh, it was Joe. He called my parents, arranged for the car to come and pick me up, and also invited me to dinner last night."

"What? I thought it was Fin who invited you to dinner."

"He knew about it, but Joe set it up." She's certain.

My mind is spinning between him flying to Dallas, jarring me out of bed, whisking me away to his brother's house, setting in motion all the other stuff regarding the house and my mom, and then last night. *I mean, Jesus, last night.* It was incredible and wasn't just protectiveness. My eyes fall on the ring. Could he really love me? Is that what he's telling me by actions and not words?

"Don't cry, Sam." Margot comes over and hugs me. "It's not a bad thing. Don't look so sad."

"He can't. It's too soon." I sob on her shoulder.

"He can, and it's not."

In the middle of our pedicures I get a text from Joseph. I shouldn't look. It's rude, but I can't help it. I'm dying to see what he said about my song.

Joseph: *That was quite a song you sent me. I'm not sure what to say. So, I'll just say this…*

Damn! He sent me a link to "Let Me Love You" by DJ Snake. He's persistent, I'll give him that. I have to up my game.

Me: *I'm not sure what you're trying to say. I think I'm missing the subtlety. Let me give you this to ponder. Maybe it will clear your head.*

I nearly chicken out, but hastily paste in the link to "Birthday Sex" by Jeremih before I lose my nerve. I laugh to myself; I seem to have a birthday theme going, which is apropos considering I just had mine.

His response comes faster than I anticipate.

Joseph: *I see how you're going to play this. I'm a determined man, Sweetness. I'm not giving up. For your listening pleasure, beautiful…*

Double damn! He's good. I click and listen to "Then There's You" by Charlie Puth. And before I even finish the first song, he texts me another one: "I Get to Love You" by Ruelle.

I start to cry when listening to that offering. He's breaking my heart already.

Margot touches my arm. "What's wrong?"

Stopping the song, I unplug my earbuds. "Joseph sent this to me."

I put my phone on speaker and start the song over. I close my eyes, laying my head back, and listen to the words, and just let the tears fall.

Margot clasps my hand in hers, closing the distance between her chair and mine by way of our joined hands.

The song surrounds me like a kaleidoscope of bright jewels dancing in my head, telling me the things I won't let him say. The things I'm afraid to hear—I'm afraid to believe.

How will I survive him?

He'll never let me keep my walls up.

He's gonna do everything he can to make me fall for him.

It's already too late.

Seven

Joseph

'M GETTING READY FOR BED WHEN MY PHONE rings. I run to catch it before it rolls to voicemail, hoping it's Samantha. It's Fin. I try not to let my disappointment seep into my voice as I answer. It's some connection with her, after all.

"Hey, how's it going?"

"Is that really what you want to ask me?"

"No." He knows me too well. "How is she?" I was all confidence and bluster today during our song texting, but truthfully, I'm anxious. I don't want to push her too fast, too hard. But, I also want her to know my intentions. I don't want to leave her with any doubt.

"She'll be alright, Joe. She just needs time to unwind. She keeps everything too close to the cuff, I wonder if she was ever really a kid. Has she ever let anyone do anything for her or has she always been in such control?"

"I think, from what she and Jace have told me, she's always been independent, self-reliant," I offer.

"The question is, is she in control because she wants to be or because she has to be? Based on her level of stress, I think it's the latter. And I don't mean to insinuate she's been neglected, but sometimes, when you have one wild child, which is Jace, in this case, and one straight arrow, such as Sam, the straight arrow is left to their own devices because they seem so capable. Perhaps it's not truly in her nature to have such control. If it was her nature, she would feed off the control and gain strength from it. In this case, though, I think the weight of the control is sapping her energy. It's taking everything she has to stay afloat, and she's come to the end of her reserves."

"You sound like a man who knows what he's talking about. Mr. Control Freak."

He laughs. "Uh, pot meet kettle."

"I learned it from the best," I say, referring to him. "I agree with your assessment. She's completely capable of being in control, but I do sense she'd rather not be, at least not always. It's been worse since her dad died, though. I'm sure feeling like she didn't have a choice in the matter makes a difference as well. When you choose to be in control, you're prepared, expecting it. This was unexpectedly dumped in her lap."

"I think the spa day was a really good idea, as well as taking to-morrow off. It'll give her a chance to recharge, refill her well, so to speak," Fin says with his typical level of confidence.

"I wish I was there." Regret fills my voice with an edge.

"You didn't have to leave."

"I did. She needs time, space. I need to give her that, and not run her over with how I'm feeling. I have a hard enough time holding back when I'm not with her, but when I'm with her, it's all consuming."

He laughs. "Yeah, I noticed that last night when you practically grabbed her by the hair and dragged her to your cave."

"I wasn't that bad." *Was I?*

"Nearly. I was hoping she'd ask me to stop you, but apparently she's fallen under your spell and actually likes your caveman ways."

I smile at the memory. "She kinda does, doesn't she?"

"Don't let it go to your head. Like you said, she needs time. I'll watch after her for you."

"Thanks, brother." I owe him one. I owe him millions by now for a lifetime of support.

"Welcome. Always."

My phone beeps, and I'm instantly pacified by the sight of her name. "Fin, she's calling."

"Go. We'll talk tomorrow." He hangs up before I can even reply.

I take a deep breath and answer.

"Sweetness." My voice is low and gruff, a voice I only use with my girl.

"Hi."

I'm happy to hear her voice, that one word holding so much emotion.

"Thank you for today. The spa, Margot, the texts, the songs. The ring. Everything," she continues quickly.

My heart fills to near bursting. "You're welcome, Samantha. Anything for you. Always."

"I miss you." She's tentative with those words, but I'm impressed she said them at all. That's not like her to be so vulnerable. I'm hoping it's a good sign in the right direction.

"I miss you too. More than you know." More than I should, or have a right to, given the state of our relationship and the distance in our future as we both finish college. I don't know how to resolve that without impacting the plans we have for our lives, our goals. I only have a year left here. Thank god she'll be here for that year. But after I graduate and return to Dallas, we're back in the same boat living in opposite cities. She has such a bright future. I can see it clearly. I can't wait to witness it. I want to be a part of it. I want to be a supporter, an encourager for her.

I take a breath. I can't solve it now. I made my choice. I'll figure it out. Make the distance work. I'm choosing to be with her now instead of waiting. "It took everything I had to leave you. I nearly turned around no less than half a dozen times," I confess. Not just because I can't stand to be away from her, but because I want to be the one by her side, keeping her safe, making her feel secure, loved, cherished.

"Really?"

She's still so uncertain about us. "Really, Samantha. Look at your finger and tell me you remember what I said."

The line is silent except for her soft breath. I picture her gazing down at her left hand, fingers splayed, admiring the ring I gave her, shining brilliantly like her beauty.

"Do you see it, Sweetness?" I wait for her to answer. I need to be sure she's with me.

"Yes." Her voice is barely audible.

"That ring of diamonds is nearly as precious as you are to me."

"You always say the sweetest things. It's hard to hear but even harder to believe." Her honesty both shocks and saddens me.

"Why do you doubt it so much?"

"God, Joseph, have you looked in the mirror? Seen what a prize you are? I've just...no one's ever seen me like you do. I expect maybe a nerd in my computer class to see me that way, but not you. Not the guy who works for my dream company, in my dream job, and treats me like I'm someone special."

"You're killing me, baby. Don't you see? I am that nerd who's sitting next to you in awe of your mind, blown away by your beauty, and kneeling at your feet asking you to love me in return."

"You're the one killing me." Her voice breaks with emotion.

"Fuck. I need to see you. Get your iPad, and I'll call you on it."

I hang up, barely giving her a chance to reply.

I power up my iPad, situating the pillows against the headboard, and get another on my lap to set the iPad on.

The moment she answers and her face appears on my screen, the air is stolen from my lungs. It's been less than twenty-four hours, and I already forgot how beautiful she truly is. I need a picture of her to remind me of that fact instead of relying on my faulty memory, which is insufficient to the task, apparently.

"God, I've missed you," I exclaim. "Look at you all cozy in bed. Sexy as hell, cute and beautiful, all at the same time."

Her smile gets bigger. "You're such a liar. I'm red and blotchy from crying. I'm a mess." She reaches out and touches the screen. "I've missed those green eyes and those dimples." Her eyes brim with tears.

"Please don't cry, baby." If she starts to cry, there's no way I won't join her when I can actually see her so full of emotions, and I'm hundreds of miles away, unable to comfort her the way I want—the way I need to. The backs of my eyes sting with the possibility of tears.

She nods. "I'm sorry. I'm a bit of a wreck." She brushes away a few tears that manage to fall. She feigns a smile, trying to mask her emotions.

"That's even more reason for you to listen to me and stop trying to fight me on this. I'm yours. You're not getting rid of me. You can fight me or you can get on board. But I'm not backing down, unless you can tell me here and now you feel nothing for me, that you don't want me to fight for our future. That you don't want me to fight for *you*."

She breaks. "Oh, god." Her sobs rip at my heart. She buries her face in her hands.

"Tell me, Sweetness. Tell me what you want. Tell me what you need and it's yours."

She raises her head, sniffling as she wipes her face. "I need you to be safe."

Christ. Fuck. That's my wish too, for her to be safe. "Do you know how scared I was when I heard you'd been shot?"

She shakes her head.

"It was like the air had been sucked from my lungs. The very life force of my being diminished with the possibility that I could lose you. Forever. No amount of planning, no amount of logical thinking could have prepared me for the vision of a life without you in it."

"But when I broke up with you…you so easily replaced me." The hurt on her face guts me.

Never. I could never replace her. How can I ever tell her the truth?

"When you broke up with me, I was right back there in that dark hole, forced to envision a future without you. I drank too much. I foolishly tried to drown my sorrow, find a reprieve from a painful reality where you married another man. Where you gave your heart to *another* man. My drinking put me in a bad place…where something incomprehensible happened."

Where I made love to you in my dream, while my body was ravaged by another.

"I can't erase what happened. I can only ask for your forgiveness and spend the rest of my life working to be the man who deserves you." One who doesn't drink himself into oblivion, putting himself at risk. I'm lucky Tiff used a condom and all tests came back negative. But I have to take responsibility for putting myself in a high-risk situation where I was not in control of my body. It's not all on me, but that part is. And that's what I have to ensure never happens again.

"It's not on you, Joseph. I'm the one who broke your heart. I started that train in motion." Her tears are back, but her eyes never waiver from mine. She's owning her part, just as I'm owning mine.

"How 'bout we share that burden? I'll forgive you, and you work on forgiving me." I suggest a compromise, as we could go all day, blaming ourselves for causing the other's pain.

She nods with a soft smile.

"Now, let's make this official. I want you to be my girlfriend. Officially. You're already wearing my ring. I want everyone to know it's *my* ring on *your* finger."

I'm so glad I can see her face. Her blue eyes stare back at me. She's biting her lower lip, and I can see her thoughts swirling around in her head.

Come on, Samantha. Say yes.

"What does that mean, exactly?" She's traded her lower lip for her thumb, capturing it between her teeth, as her eyes continue to study my face.

"It means you're mine. No one else's. It means I'm yours and no else's. Exclusive. No one touches you, and no one touches me. We make time to see each other when we can, and when we can't, we talk on the phone, text, video conference, as much as possible. It means we stop pretending this is not what it is. We embrace it and grow as a couple."

She's still just staring at me, but she's at least stopped troubling her lip and thumb. "What do you say, Sweetness? Will you be mine?"

"I think I always was, Joseph," she says softly, reverently.

A single tear streams down her cheek. I reach out to wipe it away before I realize how silly it is. "The same for me, baby. Say *yes*."

"Yes."

My smile does not even begin to reflect the joy my heart has just exploded with. "You have no idea how happy you just made me, Samantha."

"And you're really mine? *Only* mine?" She casts her eyes downward, like she can't bear to see me if I say *no*.

"Look at me."

Tears well up as she focuses on the screen.

"Baby, why does that upset you?"

Her chin starts to tremble. "I'm sorry I keep crying, Joseph." She averts her eyes as she wipes the tears that continue to fall.

"Please, look at me."

She raises her chin, her eyes back on mine.

"That's better. I don't like it when you hide from me. You don't need to apologize for being emotional, especially not after all that's happened. Tell me why you're crying."

Her voice cracks as she replies. "Because no one's ever been mine before, and no one has ever *wanted* me to be theirs."

There it is. That insecurity of being a supposed leper. Damn, Jace.

"It's a first for me too, Sweetness. I've dated, but I've never met anyone I wanted to be exclusive with, not until you. To answer your question, yes, I'm 100% yours, only yours. Exclusively."

She smiles, and then yawns as she wipes the last of her tears.

"It's late. I should let you get to bed." I kept her up late last night.

"I don't want to let you go, not yet. Can we talk for just a few minutes more?"

That pleases me endlessly. "Yes. Lie down and put me on the bed next to you like I'm lying there with you."

We both lie down, placing our tablets in the place the other person's head would be if we were in bed together. She settles in, flipping her hair up over the pillow, pulling the covers up. I can see her from the shoulders up, sexy and adorable. It's a heady combination.

The conversation flows easily. It always has between us. Natural. Unforced. Home.

She's my home.

Samantha is not someone who needs to be talking all the time, or have social interaction, or attention lavished on her. She's more of a loner when it comes to that sort of thing. She prefers not to be in the limelight. She's definitely not like her brother in that respect, who loves to be the center of attention.

She yawns again.

"Baby, you're so tired, close your eyes. I'll stay on the line until you fall asleep, or until your screen times out."

She smiles sleepily. "I wish you were here to hold me, keep me warm, make me feel safe and taken care of."

"I wish I was there, too. But I promise you are safe and taken care of. Now blow me a kiss and close your eyes."

She blows me a kiss and flashes me a dreamy smile. "Thank you, Joseph, for today. For my ring, for forgiving me for my birthday lie."

"You're welcome and forgiven. I'm sorry I didn't understand what you really needed for your birthday. I'll endeavor to do better. To give you what you really need and not what I think you need." I blow her a kiss back. "Now, close your eyes. Call me tomorrow."

"Okay. Goodnight, Joseph."

"Goodnight, Sweetness."

She settles further into her pillow, letting out a deep breath, fidgeting just a moment, before she stills and her eyes slowly start to close. She fights it, but eventually her body wins out, and she falls asleep. I stay on the line, watching her sleep, dreaming of the day I'll be there beside her in person every night, not just occasionally.

When her screen finally goes black and the call ends, I whisper, "Goodnight, my sweet girl." I close my tablet, roll over and turn off the lights, settling in for a better night's sleep than I anticipated getting.

Samantha

Despite having the luxury of sleeping in, I wake up at seven, which is sleeping in for me, but not as long as I had hoped. I could roll over and probably go back to sleep, but decide it's better to just get up. I'm anxious to get my day of relaxation started. I throw on yoga pants and a t-shirt, just getting myself decent enough to walk around Fin and not embarrass myself, or him.

When I open the door, the amazing smell of coffee reaches me all the way down the hall. I walk into the kitchen and stop.

Fin's there with his back to me, wearing a pair of workout shorts. Nothing else. He's fit. Really fit. Seeing him like this only makes me think of Joseph, though. Fin's good-looking with the same dark hair and remarkable green eyes as Joseph, and a body no one would throw out of bed, but he's not my Joseph. Joseph is taller, more muscular, broader, and has thicker thighs. Fin is a leaner version of Joseph. If they were athletes, Fin has the swimmer's body, and Joseph is the football player.

He turns, surprising me.

"Hi," I say before he catches me staring at him.

"Oh, hey." He stills, surprised to see me. "I thought you'd still be asleep." He grabs the towel on the counter and dabs at the sweet on his body. "Sorry, I just worked out and wanted to grab a cup of coffee before showering."

I avert my eyes. "It's your home, Fin. You don't need to apologize. I'm sorry I startled you." I point to the coffee. "Do you mind if I get a cup?"

"No, of course." He hands me a mug from the nearby cabinet. "There's creamer in the fridge and sugar is right there." He points to the carafe sitting next to the fancy coffee maker.

I still when I get a good look at the contraption in front of me. "Fin, do I need a license to operate this?"

He chuckles as he comes over to help me out. "No, but it did take me a few weeks to conquer it." He takes the mug from me. "Here let me show you."

He demonstrates how to pour a plain cup of coffee, and how to use the plethora of other functions as well. In the end, I end up with a French vanilla cappuccino that smells to die for.

I take a tentative sip, not wanting to burn my mouth. "Holy shit. This is amazing." I look back at the machine and then at him. "You should marry her. Don't let her get away."

He laughs. "Don't think I haven't considered it."

I open the fridge, taking out the bacon and eggs he showed me last night. "If I make breakfast, would you eat before you leave?"

The awe on his face makes me wish he had someone to cook for him every day. "Absolutely."

As he heads off to the shower, I think how lonely it must be up here. "Fin, would it be alright to call Matt and see if he wants to join us?"

When Fin doesn't respond, I figure he didn't hear me. Then his voice sounds from down the hall. "I'll call and invite him. Go ahead and plan on it."

"Okay." Before I do anything else I run to my room and grab my iPad. I set it on the counter and call Joseph. I want to see him before I start my day.

"Sweetness. This is a nice surprise. I didn't expect to hear from you, much less see you this morning." His voice is sexy and still gruff from sleep.

"I took a chance you'd be up." I disappear out of the frame. "I hope you don't mind if we chat while I work." I come back and adjust the tablet to angle toward the stove.

"What are you doing?" His neck cranes as if he can control the angle of my iPad just by his movements.

"I'm making breakfast for your brothers." I glance up just long enough to see him smile.

"That's really nice of you. Matt's coming over too?" He seems surprised.

"Yes, I thought it was weird me being here and not offering to make him breakfast too, given he's just across the hall."

"If he is across the hall," Joseph replies.

"Where else would he be…" Then it dawns on me. "Oh, you mean—"

"Yeah, he may have slept out." He runs his fingers through his hair.

I brush off the thought as I put the bacon on the cookie sheet for the oven. "It's no big deal. I'll eat whatever is left later." I glance up at him. "What's your day like today? Do you need to leave?"

"No class today, remember? I'm heading to a study group."

That's right, it's Friday. I've lost track of my days. "If you need to go, it's okay. I just wanted to say hi." I peer over my shoulder at his framed, handsomely sleepy face. "I wanted to see you, even if only for a minute."

His dimpled grin makes my heart race. "It's good to see you too. And I don't need to go quite yet, but I'll finish getting ready while you cook for my brothers, whom I'm jealous of right now, by the way."

I did cook him bacon and eggs the night of my dad's funeral. It would be a sad memory, except for how much he and Jace seemed to enjoy the home cooking. "I'll cook for you anytime you're in town, Joseph." I put the bacon in the oven and get out what is needed for the eggs. I hear noises but no Joseph on the screen. "Hey, are you getting naked?"

His face pops back on. "Do you want me to get naked?" I can see the gleam in his eye and his bare chest. Close enough to naked for me to appreciate what I'm missing.

"Well, I'm not sure how your brothers would feel about walking into the kitchen and seeing you in your birthday suit."

"Good point, another time then." He laughs as he disappears off the screen again. "Getting my shoes, be right back."

"Hey, is that coffee I smell?" Matt's voice precedes his appearance in the kitchen, but not by much. He smiles when he sees me. "Good morning. Thanks for the invite to breakfast, Sam."

"You're welcome. I'm glad you could join us." I break eggs in a bowl.

"What can I do to help?" Matt offers.

"How about plates and silverware?" I suggest.

"On it." Matt moves with determination to complete the task at hand. All of the McIntyre men seem to have a single-minded focus of slaying whatever tasks lies ahead of them.

"Hey, Matt."

Matt jumps. I stifle my laugh in my shoulder. I guess I should've warned him we weren't alone.

Wide-eyed, Matt scans the kitchen. "Joe?"

"Here, man, on the island." Joseph's voice fills the kitchen again.

Matt turns the iPad to face him. "Hey. Shit, you scared me. I wasn't expecting to hear your voice."

They chat for few minutes as I cook the eggs and get the bread in the toaster. Before too long, Fin joins us in the kitchen, dapper in his well-tailored navy slacks and white button-down with his tie and jacket in hand. He joins Joseph and Matt in conversation as I plate up breakfast. Matt is dressed similarly, except in dark charcoal pants. Matt and Fin's suit jackets and ties are slung over the back of the couch, waiting to be donned to finish out their business armor for the day.

I set the plates on the breakfast bar and hear my name. I turn to the three of them. Matt and Fin face me, shoulder to shoulder, the same height, and Matt's holding my iPad displaying Joseph's grinning face. Three sets of identical green eyes staring back at me. "Samantha, let me have a minute with you alone before you eat."

I take my tablet from Matt and excuse myself, exiting to my room. "What's up?" I ask on my way down the hall.

"I just wanted to say goodbye to you in private, without my eavesdropping brothers around."

I close the bedroom door and sit on the nearest chair, holding Joseph on my lap. "Okay, we're alone."

His eyes scan my face like he hasn't seen me in years. "Thank you for calling this morning. I don't think I realized how much I needed to hear your voice and see your lovely face today."

My heart skips a beat. "Joseph, you're going to make my cry if you keep being so nice to me."

"Well, then I guess you'll just have to cry, because I'm not going to stop telling you how much you mean to me or how I'm thankful you thought to call me this morning."

I'm glad such a simple thing makes him happy. "It's good to see your handsome face too, but honestly, I think it makes me miss you more."

"It's a good thing I get to see you soon then, for spring break."

"What do you mean?" I'm shocked. "Are you coming home for spring break? I thought you and Jace were going on a trip."

"I'm coming to see you, Sweetness."

"Joseph." I have to close my eyes to stop from crying.

"Open your eyes, beautiful. Let me see those baby-blues I love so much."

He loves my eyes?

I open them. His gaze is soft. "There they are. You don't have to try not to cry with me, Samantha. I'm not Jace. I'm not going to call them your *girly emotions* and make you feel bad about them. Whatever you feel, I want to know it. I want to see it."

I nod and wipe away my tears. "When will I see you?"

He thinks for a moment. "I'm not sure yet, the Saturday before the break, for sure."

"I'd like that."

"Me too." He flashes his watch. "I gotta go. I'll call you later. Enjoy your day and know I wish I was with you."

"Me too. Bye, Joseph."

"Bye, Sweetness."

Eight

Samantha

AFTER A DAY OF NO SCHOOL OR WORK, I'M GOING stir crazy. I can't sit around Fin's place one more minute. Yesterday's spa day was alright as I was busy doing something, even though it was relaxing and not work or school related. But after Fin and Matt left for work, sitting around Fin's not knowing what to do with myself is a feeling I'm not comfortable with. I'm not good with idle time, and too much time to think is not a good thing for me, at least not right now. I don't want to focus on my father's death, the school work I'm missing, or how much I miss Joseph. It's only been two days, and it feels like weeks.

My options are limited. Everyone is either at work or school. On a whim, I call Sebastian. Maybe he's off today or has a late shift.

"Hey, how's the prettiest friend I have?" his silky voice oozes over the phone.

"Bash, you know I hate it when you lay it on thick like that. Who talks like that, really?"

"I do, babycakes. If you hung out with me more, you'd know that," he admonishes.

"If you're available, we could remedy that over lunch."

"Done. Where?" He jumps on that idea rather quickly.

"Um, I'm downtown. Any place you recommend between here and wherever you are?"

He laughs. "Why are you downtown? And why aren't you in school?"

"I'll tell you all about it over lunch."

"Are you playing hooky? Are you going to ask me to forge a parent note?"

"Seriously?" I'm not really upset, but it's fun to push his buttons. He always comes circling back quickly with his comforting, flirtatious way of his. He wouldn't dare let me go a minute without knowing he's 100% behind me, whatever it is.

"I can't think of any other reason you'd be out of school and still be okay to have lunch. You're obviously not sick, at least not physically."

"Oh gee, thanks."

"I'm kidding, beautiful. I know you're physically sick too." He busts out laughing, and I can't help but join him.

We agree on a place to meet. What should I do from here? Do I go on my own, or do I call Michael or Victor? I decide to text both of them and see what they say.

I toss my phone on my bed and quickly get ready. When I come out of the bathroom, there's texts from both of them informing me that Victor will be up shortly to collect me.

Collect. Me.

That cracks me up, like I'm garbage or laundry to be collected and carted away.

"Enough of the pleasantries. Fill me in, Sam. What's going on?" Sebastian discreetly motions to the guy who walked in with me and then proceeded to sit two tables over from us, looking like he's studying the menu, but I'm sure he's actually checking out the room behind those dark shades he's wearing.

"Just ignore him. I doubt he's the only one in here. I'm not supposed to notice them, but I can feel 'em watching me."

He gives me a stern glare. "Spill it, babycakes. What the fuck?"

"Do you talk to your patients with that mouth?" I smile and try to make light of the situation.

"I do lots of things with this mouth, the least of which will be to unleash its full verbal potential on you if you don't start talkin." He's not kidding. Nice, laid-back Sebastian has taken a backseat to overprotective, concerned Sebastian.

"Okay…" As I start to fill him in, it dawns on me, perhaps we shouldn't be discussing this in public. It would have been a better idea to have him come to the penthouse. I imagine Joseph would prefer a public meeting—and I needed to get out of the house.

I wrap up the drama of the last few weeks, feeling bad we haven't spoken, but it was part of my plan to keep everyone I care about safe. Bash is no exception. Though we haven't been friends long, he's become important to me. He doesn't have any preconceived notions of who I am. He doesn't let me fall into my self-doubt, and he most definitely can't go more than a few minutes without reminding me how beautiful and special he thinks I am. I love that about him.

He may wish we were intimately involved and not just friends, but he cherishes our friendship too. He doesn't really have any female friends. He's the typical sex god with tons of macho male friends, and the only women in his life are either related to him or date him. I'm the first woman to turn down his overt flirtations, and I stand out in his mind, in his life because I'm not the typical pushover who falls for his charms. I see to the heart of who he is under all his boastful confidence and preening.

He reaches out and takes my hand. "Fuck, Sam. Seriously? You should have called me sooner. I would have been there for you, especially after the Joseph thing." He squeezes my hand gently. "That must have broken your heart. I can't believe he slept with someone else."

My stomach churns. "I shouldn't have told you that. It's not fair to him. He didn't do anything wrong. I'd broken up with him. He was…" I look away nearly in tears.

"Heartbroken." Bash gives voice to what I can't bear to say.

"Yeah, and apparently really drunk." I wave the vision away. "Anyway, we both have regrets, and we're working through it." I take a long sip of iced tea.

His hand brushes my cheek. "Do you want me to talk to him?"

I shake my head adamantly. "God, no. I doubt he'd be happy I told you. I really shouldn't have. I'm sorry." This learning to share thing is hard. I don't want to betray Joseph's confidence, but if I don't talk about it, how do I learn to let people in? How can I share my life without any details? It's obviously a fine line I'm going to have to learn to navigate.

"You don't need to apologize. You were telling a friend in confidence what's been going on with you, and that's a pretty big chunk of your news. I'm not happy with what he did, but I'll reserve my judgments based on how you're handling it. And right now, you're telling me he didn't cheat on you because you were broken up at the time, so I'll accept it until I know otherwise."

"Thanks. I don't want to impact your view of him—your relationship. It's important to me that you two get along."

"It won't, but I'm your friend first. So, if there are sides to pick—"

"There aren't." My eyes search out his. "But, if there were, you should pick his side. I was the one who hurt him first. It's my fault what happened."

"Sam," he castigates, getting ready to admonish me for my self-deprecation.

"Don't. Please. Let's just drop it and enjoy our lunch. Okay?"

He stares at me for the longest time. I wait patiently for him to come around to my way of thinking or at least acceptance of it.

"Okay." His soft acquiescence is nearly lost in the din of the restaurant.

"Thank you."

He gives me a curt nod. "Welcome." He points to my food. "Eat. I can tell you haven't been taking care of yourself. You eat, and I'll entertain you with my latest patient escapades." The mischief in his eyes and playful smirk make me relax.

All at once I'm thankful for having met Bash and his easy way of lightening my load. He's a gift. A true gift, and I can't wait till he finds the woman who's strong enough to love him. I nearly get lost in my rumination of what this woman will be like and if she and I will get along, when he brings me back with his next line.

"I finally convinced him to drop trou and show me the problem." I can tell by the gleam in his eye this is going to be good. "I kid you not, Sam. He had a fucking eel attached to his johnson."

I spit the mouthful of tea I was foolish enough to take a drink of mid-story. I manage to turn my head just enough to only spew it across the side of the table and over his left arm.

"Oh, crap! I'm so sorry." I start to mop up the table and him, mortified by the looks the other customers give me.

He's laughing so hard, he doesn't even care I spit sweet tea all over him, or at least a part of him. He swishes my hands away. "It's fine, babycakes." He uses his napkin to wipe himself off. "I'm an ER doctor. I'm used to being covered in other people's bodily fluids."

I nearly gag. "Bash! Uh, that's just gross."

He chuckles. "Tell me about it." He settles back in his chair, checking me out. "You okay?" Ever the doctor, needing to be sure I didn't hurt myself choking on iced tea.

I dab my mouth, clothes, and my side of the table. "Yeah, you just took me by surprise. I wasn't choking." He glances in question at my shoulder. "It's fine."

He drops the concerned look and gets back to his story. "You think you're surprised? I yelled in horror when I saw a long black thing just hanging from his...dick. I thought it was a huge leech at first."

I lean forward. "Please tell me it wasn't still alive." Poor eel.

"That's what you want to know? Not how it got there in the first place?" His face is lit with amusement.

"I already surmised why he wanted an eel on his... So, my next thought was, was it alive when it happened, and did you have to kill it trying to get it off?"

"Baby, I did not get the man off." His hands cross in a motion as if he's an ump calling a runner "safe." "In fact, just the vision of it is enough to make me sustain from getting off for some time to come."

I think he's totally serious. "You're joking, right?"

He smirks. "Well, partially. But, it's a vision I'm gonna have to work to wipe from my mind every time I touch my cock." He cringes. "Sorry."

Bash doesn't talk sexually to me. *Ever*. He's succeeded at keeping our friendship as, well, just that…friends. He's naturally flirty, but rarely mentions sex or sexual body parts. Though, I'm not sure if it's the whole friendship thing or him trying to protect my innocence.

"You know I'm an adult, right? You don't have to shy away from talking about sex or penises and vaginas. I can handle it."

He shrugs. "I'm trying to be good here and not go into dangerous territory not covered by the friendship clause."

So, he's not protecting my innocence, but our friendship. "Bash, really? Even friends talk about sex. Are you telling me you don't talk about sex and body parts with your male friends?"

He leans closer. "That's different, and you know it. I don't want to have sex with them."

"Bash—"

His hand goes up, stopping me mid-thought. "I cherish our friendship, Sam. But you know I don't see you as a sister. I never have. I never will. We may never be more than friends, but it doesn't mean I'm not still attracted to the sexy, smart, witty woman sitting across from me." He raises his eyebrow in emphasis, waiting for my acknowledgment. Once again, he wants me to accept his compliment without brushing it off.

I grab his hand and squeeze, trying to hide the tears in my eyes. This man is too sweet to me. "You honor me with your words. Your reverence of our friendship, and your respect of my relationship with Joseph." I hold his gaze momentarily, but I can't keep eye contact if I have any hope of not crying. "You're an amazing man, Sebastian Cole. I can't wait to meet the woman who's worthy of your heart."

"Sam." His voice is heavy with emotion now.

The room is bustling around us, but there's a moment of peace and quiet between us. We know where we stand. We respect it and each other enough to be honest. I meet his eyes. I see the beautiful man behind his model-handsome face. "I *see* you, Bash. Don't ever forget that."

His eyes glisten, making my tears overflow their confinement. "I see you too, beautiful. And don't *you* ever forget that."

As I dab my tears, he proceeds to tell me the eel was alive when it became attached, but had long since died from lack of oxygen. Sad, so sad for that poor eel.

"Where in the hell did he get an eel?" PETA should be called in to investigate. It's a travesty. *Okay, maybe I'm over reacting a little, but seriously. A fucking eel?*

"He wouldn't tell me. He was afraid of getting fired from his job. So, I did *my* job and removed the appendage from his gnarled and heinously unimpressive man-meat."

A horrendous thought hits me. Bash doesn't miss the flash of disgust on my face. "What?"

"Please tell me he wasn't planning on...uh...having sex with that thing still attached to him."

He frowns. "You mean as in a slip-on eel dildo to enhance his size?"

"Yes." I shudder at the thought and the poor recipient of such a gift.

"Fuck. Jeez, I surely hope not. Thanks for that visual." He shakes his head to dispel the thought. "We didn't talk much more after he clammed up about where he got the eel in the first place. Psych came and talked to him. I pretty much just focused on the immediate issue of removal and salvage."

A whole-body shudder takes over at the thought. "I think your story just may have ruined sex for me."

He laughs.

I point at him. "You won't be laughing when Joseph calls to ask why you filled my mind with such horrible imagery and ruined any chance he had of popping my cherry."

His head falls back, and a deep, full-body laugh escapes. "Like you'd ever be able to resist him for long. I see the way you two look at each other. It's a miracle you've lasted this long."

"It is, isn't it?"

We near the end of our meal, and I know he has to get back to the hospital. He's working a split shift today, so he only had a little time to spare. I'm thankful he wasted it on me. I excuse myself and head to the restroom before we leave.

I do my business and head back to the table.

And then I see him.

The man who shot my father and me, and tore my family apart.

I nearly miss my chair as I stumble back into my seat. I take a long drink and try to calm my nerves, hoping I look casual, natural instead of completely terrified. Did the security team fail, or was this man here already, the universe conspiring against me to make this moment happen?

"Sam?" Bash sees there's something wrong. "What…"

I stab at my food. "Don't look around. I need you to make a phone call for me."

"You're scaring me, Sam."

I reach across and squeeze his hand. I'm the world's biggest asshole for putting my friend in danger because I selfishly thought I needed a day out of the penthouse. It's been days, not months. Why didn't I stay there where it's safe? Where everyone else was safe—far away from me. "Please," I whisper so softly I'm not sure Bash hears me.

With a squeeze in return, he asks me the number. I automatically dictate the number Michael forced me to memorize. He was insistent I know his number by heart. I guess this is a perfect example as to why.

"Why aren't you using your phone?" Bash asks as he puts the phone to his ear.

"I don't want him to know I saw him."

Bash starts to say something, but stops when Michael answers. I can hear his voice coming through the phone. "Sebastian. What's wrong?"

I dig through the packet of sugars as if I'm trying to find the magical one I need. "He's here," I simply say.

Bash starts to repeat, but I guess Michael can hear me too and cuts off Bash's reply. "Where?"

"Back left corner of the bar." I purposely focus in the opposite direction, pointing at a paining on the wall as if I'm telling Sebastian something about it.

"Don't move," Michael orders before he hangs up.

If anything happens to Sebastian because I invited him to lunch, I'll never forgive myself. My heart pounds, and I meet Sebastian's steely gaze for the first time since returning from the bathroom.

"I'm sorry," I softly impart, barely two seconds before all hell breaks loose.

PART 4
HEAR ME ROAR
APRIL

Nine

Samantha

I N A FLASH, EVERYTHING CHANGED. I WAS YOUR average girl-next-door who studied too much, worked too hard, and rarely had any fun. The only notable male interaction in my life was with my father, my brother, or my co-workers, none of whom wanted to date me. I then watched my father die in my arms, survived being shot, dated, lost, and then again dated the hottest man I've ever seen.

To say he's hot is not even fair—and doesn't do him justice. It makes him sound like a one-dimensional Ken doll with nothing between his ears whom I only appreciate for his physical beauty. While it is true I do appreciate every inch of his body, he is, in fact, the smartest man I know. His brain, his heart, and even his caveman ways are all a part of the man I've grown to love.

I said I wouldn't fall in love with him. But it was a lost cause from the moment I laid eyes on him that Friday Jace introduced us. I was a fool for believing I could resist his charm, his steady green-eyed gaze, and all-consuming presence. I thought he would leave me heartbroken and devastated.

Well, I *am* heartbroken. I *am* devastated. But, not from Joseph. I am broken from losing my father, my mother, and my brother in one fell swoop. Though I haven't physically lost my mom and brother, their absence in my life is just as true as the loss of my father, with one exception. My mom and brother *chose* to shut me out of their lives. My father didn't have a choice.

Joseph is the one picking up the pieces, holding me together, comforting me, giving me strength, and giving me a safe place to land. He's been my saving grace.

My godsend.

My protector.

My healer.

My teacher.

My confidant.

My rock.

My heart.

My breath.

My soul.

He picked me up when I didn't deserve it. He healed my brokenness and set me free.

"Sam!" Michael snaps at me.

I whirl around and face him. "What?"

"Where the hell were you?" He sighs, exasperated with me as he wipes sweat off his face and arms. "Are you ready to go again?"

I take one more long drink of water and then head for the center of the mat. "Bring it, asswipe."

He chuckles. "You only cuss at me. Why is that?"

I love it when I can make stoic Michael—always serious Michael—laugh. I shrug. "I don't know. You bring out the best in me, I suppose."

He assumes his fight stance opposite me. "Well, let's see if you can take me down this time."

"If I do, you have to answer any question I ask you honestly, and not a one-word answer. You have to give me a complete, truthful, no-bullshit answer."

His eyes narrow as he gives me the evil, take-no-shit glare of his. "And if you don't take me down? What do I get?"

"What do you want?"

A mischievous smirk reduces his glare to a decisive squint as his eyes sweep up and down my body. "A favor."

I step back and cross my arms over my chest. "What kind of favor?"

He laughs again, reading me like a book. "Not *that* kind of favor. Get your head out of the gutter."

"What kind, then?"

He shrugs. "I don't know yet. But I kinda like the idea of you owing me something. Something I can collect on at anytime, anywhere, and you can't say no."

It's a sobering thought of how much I already owe this man. He's doing his job, protecting me, keeping me out of harm's way. He's gone above and beyond to help Joseph and me. I don't know all the facts, but I see the looks, I hear bits and pieces of conversations. He's fully invested in me and my family's safety, and that's a debt I can never repay.

And if that wasn't enough, he and Victor have been working with me for the past month teaching me self-defense moves based on kick boxing and jujitsu techniques. Michael is a fourth-degree black belt. Victor never went the formal route. What he learned was from his years in the military and as MCI's head of security. He may not have black belt status, but he can kick ass all the same.

"Michael, I already owe you. I couldn't possibly owe you any more than I already do. If you ever have anything you need from me in the future, you don't have to collect a favor. I owe a debt to you I can never repay. So, whatever you need, it's yours. Pick something else for our wager."

He steps close enough to touch my arm, just grazing it, before letting his hand fall to his side. "You don't own me a damn thing, princess. It's my job, my honor, to protect you and keep you safe." He moves back into position. "The wager stays the same. You won't owe me for protecting you, but you'll owe me one favor, anything, for not taking me down. Now, come on, show me what you got, little miss bookworm."

Thirty seconds later, I'm flat on my back, Michael is hovering over me with a totally satisfied smirk.

"Crap!"

He shakes his head and gives me a hand up. "Again."

Fifteen minutes later, I'm completely winded and only managed to knock him off balance, but not off his feet. "Jesus, what are you, a weeble-wobble?"

"As in *weebles wobble, but they don't fall down?*" he chuckles.

"Yes! Fuck. Seriously. I almost had you, but you refuse to fall down!" I stomp toward him and push him hard on his chest. He doesn't fucking budge.

His face softens. "You've done really well, Sam. Don't get discouraged. I've been at this for a long time. What kind of ex-military, FBI agent would I be if you could take me down after only four weeks of training?"

"A damn good instructor! That's what you'd be." I sigh and grab my water. "Are we done?"

Glancing at the clock, he nods. "Yeah, take a breather. Let me clean up here, then I'll take you home."

I swipe my towel and my gym bag as I head out front.

We're in an unmarked gym across town from Fin's. I have no clue what goes on here during the day, but whenever we come to train in the evenings, it's completely empty except for Michael, me, sometimes Victor, and the other agents assigned to me. It's fully equipped with treadmills, ellipticals, free weights, punching bags, dummies, wall-to-wall mats, and three boxing rings dispersed throughout. I've asked questions, but Michael's not giving up any details. It's like it's a secret society or something.

I've learned to choose my battles. I'm safe here, the doors are locked, security system is engaged, and there are more agents roaming around than I could possibly need. I'm not complaining, though. I remain thankful for the feeling of security it affords me. That security has been extended to the rest of my family and Joseph's as a precaution. I've agreed to stay away from Margot and Sebastian, especially after what happened the last time I saw Bash.

It's been four weeks since the scare at the restaurant with Sebastian and seeing my dad's killer there. Michael and his team came in like

SWAT, ready to take down the place, but somehow the weasel managed to slip away. I felt guilty, like maybe I imagined the whole thing. I was thankful when Michael told me later, after watching the security tapes, the killer had, in fact, been there. I was relieved until I realized how much danger we were in and what could have happened. He was mere feet from me when I went to the restroom. He could have grabbed me or hurt Sebastian to get to me.

"You ready?" Michael stands near the door, his gym bag slung over his shoulder. His gun is holstered, secured at his hip once again.

"Yeah." I roll my shoulders, trying to release the tension.

On the way home we stop for food from a drive-thru. One thing I really like about Michael, is his love of Jack-in-the-Box monster tacos. He has a serious addiction that rivals my own. He ordered eight monster tacos to my two, onion rings, and two large cokes.

Food in hand, we step off the elevator. He drops our gym bags outside Fin's door, but instead of going inside, he moves to the door around the corner I'd assumed was a closet or storage of some sort. Apparently, it's a stairwell.

He holds the door open, motioning me through.

"Where are we going?" I start to climb the stairs.

The door shuts behind him with a soft clasp instead of the echoing boom I expect from most stairwell doors. "You'll see. Come on, slowpoke," he teases as he races up the stairs ahead of me.

My legs wobble like rubber as I make the ascent to the roof. The rooftop pool, that is. "Holy shit. This is incredible."

"I'm surprised Joe hasn't brought you up here."

"Me too." After the restaurant incident, Joseph couldn't fly home to my side fast enough. It took me a week to get him to go home to Austin with a begrudgingly made promise to stay away, at least for the interim. I'm not sure if it was me or Fin, Michael, or Victor who finally talked some sense into him. Whatever it was, he finally went home with his own security team in tow—that was for *my* peace of mind.

His absence is hardly bearable, but I need that extra knowledge he's hundreds of miles away. I've been keeping to myself, barely working, only going to school and home to Fin's. I can't stand the idea of getting anyone hurt because of me, and that includes those whose job is to protect me. It's not forever. The solitude is temporary, and really, other than Joseph, it's not any great sacrifice. It's in my nature, and I'm feeding that lone beast quite regularly.

I move closer to the pool's edge. It's beautiful and tranquil with the shimmering light just below the surface. I resist the urge to jump in.

Michael sets down our food and drinks at a table surrounded by blooming potted plants.

Spring. I forgot it was spring already.

We eat in companionable silence. I wasn't always at ease around him, but over the last month, Michael has pretty much become my daily companion. Except when I'm in school or working, one of the other guys is stuck to me like glue, but any other time, it's Michael at my side. We eat together. We watch TV together. We even read together. I never pictured him a reader, but he enjoys pretty much anything as long as it's not a romance. He learned to appreciate a good book in the military. There was a lot of down time, waiting for orders, or waiting for someone or something to happen. He always has a paperback on him, either in his bag or in his back pocket.

I swipe an onion ring from him. He chuckles and pushes them between us. I finished my tacos in record time, starving after our training session and my physical therapy I had before that. I'm thankful it's Friday. I can't wait to shower, my new guilty pleasure thanks to the penthouse's decadent showers, then crawl into bed and not wake up until my eyes open on their own, sans alarm clock.

Michael draws a napkin across his mouth, wipes his hands, then collects our trash and disposes of it in the nearest trashcan. He comes back and sits in the same seat, but his focus is now on me instead of slaying his mound of monster tacos.

"What?" I wonder if I have food on my face, but I'm pretty sure I managed to wipe all the greasy goodness off.

"Ask me."

My brow furrows as I try to surmise what the hell he's talking about. "Ask what?"

"Your question. Our wager." He states it so simply, like I should have known what he was talking about.

"But I didn't win. You did. You get your favor, which you didn't need in the first place." I roll my eyes in mock dismissal of his claiming "it's his honor" to protect me. *Shit.* It's enough to make me cry. He's a good man. Tortured, but good.

"It doesn't matter. You earned it." He tips his chin. "One question. One full disclosure answer."

"Seriously?"

"Seriously." He clasps his hands behind his head and leans back in the chair. "Ask."

I don't have to even think about *what* I want to ask, but I do have to think about *how* to ask it.

His arched brow and the rocking of his chair balancing on two legs tell me he's nearly done waiting on me.

"Okay." I take a deep breath and decide to go for it. "When I look at you, Michael, I see a strong man who's seen his fair share of bad things, probably horrific things. I see the soldier you used to be, the agent you are, the loyal friend, the protector, the guy who wants to have a beer and watch TV, and the quiet guy who likes to get lost in a book. I've seen many sides of you, and I'm sure there's more. The one thing I want to know is what happened to put that longing in your eyes? The memories that steal your smile. The devastation that damaged your spirit."

His smug look disappears as his chair slams down on the cobble-stone patio. "Fuck." His hands wash across his face. Leaning forward, he plucks a flower from the pot near his foot, before his arms come to rest on his knees.

I'm not sure he's going to answer me. The longer I wait, the more likely it is he'll brush off my question, or maybe it's a good sign he hasn't blown me off yet. A sign he's contemplating an answer instead of formulating a lie.

"I should have known it wouldn't be an easy question." His voice is heavy with emotion. His sad eyes measure mine, wondering if I can take what he's about to say. "I'll tell you what I can, but I can't tell you all of it or give you specifics. Not because I'm lying to you, but partly because I can't legally, and mostly because it's not my story to tell."

Jesus. This is gonna be heavy. Maybe I should have asked him my cop-out question: *What's your favorite sexual position?* It would have been an easier question for sure, but not nearly as meaningful. I have a feeling this is a burden he needs to share, and I'm willing to listen. I want to know more about the man I've spent so much time with lately and is such good friends with Victor and Fin. He's more than his gruff façade—that I know for certain.

He sits back in his chair, his hands gripping the arm rests and his eyes boring into me. "I was undercover a few years ago. Investigating a real scumbag. The kind of guy whose death would be too kind a punishment. He was dirty in a lot of ways, used people, manipulated innocent people who lost their way. If you can imagine the things a charismatic lowlife, morally corrupt, pompous asshole might enjoy, he did it and worse."

His eyes cloud as he gazes out over the pool. "Sometimes—actually most times—when you're undercover, you have to do things you wouldn't normally do to maintain your cover and get closer to the suspect. This job was no different. I'm not proud of what I did, the compromises I made, but I wouldn't do it any differently. I wouldn't change a damn thing as it brought me my Gracie, and it put him away for life."

My Gracie. Jeez. I'm gonna cry.

"She wasn't supposed to be there. If I'd known what he had planned, I would have intervened, but it all happened so quick." He closes his eyes and shakes his head as if to dispel the unpleasant memory.

"Anyway, I ran interference. I tried to distract him. I did everything I could to keep him away from her for as long as I could. But..." His voice cracks, and a beat passes before he continues. "I couldn't jeopardize the investigation. If I hadn't been in so deep, if we weren't so close to making an arrest, I would have just left and taken her with me. But I couldn't. I had to choose."

He clears his throat. "I chose my job. I chose the greater good over her. The sacrifice of one for the many."

"That's what you were trained to do. To sacrifice for the greater good." I'm sure it's little solace for the guilt he feels.

"Yes." He nods. "A good soldier follows orders, doesn't rock the boat. Doesn't put the needs of an individual over the needs of the masses. But I should have put her needs over all else. I should have taken her and slipped away in the night. I could have saved her. Protected her innocence."

Shit.

He eyes lock with mine. "What if she was meant to do amazing things and because of this horrible incident, she doesn't do it? Aren't the masses impacted anyway? Maybe the needs of the one should take precedence over the needs of the many because the future masses are impacted if the one is derailed in some way."

"Michael, you don't know that. Nobody does. All we can do is make the best decision we can at the time based on the facts we have at that moment. You can't spend your life second-guessing yourself. It won't change the past, and it may, in fact, change your future because you're too busy looking back to look forward."

He seems to contemplate for a moment. I want to know what happened to her, but I'm afraid to ask. I don't want to dredge up more pain than he's already feeling.

"You loved her."

"Yeah."

Then I realize. "You *still* love her."

His eyes meet mine. "Yeah, I do."

Michael. He's breaking my heart. "How'd she get away from him?"

"I snuck her out." He sits back in his chair, washing his face with his hand again and lets out a long breath.

"In the end, I did choose her. Better late than never, I guess." He shrugs. "I snuck her out early in the morning and hid her on the grounds far from the main compound. I had to go back and collect evidence, set a smoke screen to keep her escape a secret for as long as possible. What I had no way of knowing was that her boyfriend and his family connections got the FBI to raid the place about an hour later."

He lets out a bitter laugh. "She would have been saved anyway. In the end, what I did didn't mean crap."

"I don't believe that. You chose her. She knows that. She might've been hurt in the raid if you hadn't gotten her out. What you did made a difference. It kept her safe." *What if she did get hurt?*

"Yes, she was safe and out of danger. I was making my way back to get her, when her boyfriend and other agents found her."

Oh shit! "What'd ya do?"

"The only thing I could. I sent her home with the man who could love her better than I could."

"Michael, that's heartbreaking." I quietly wipe away an errant tear.

He peers out over the night sky, and I think he's done talking. Then he surprises me. "You have no idea."

I do actually. I have some idea what it's like to let go of the one you love because you believe they're better off without you. Safer without you. I did it, and it broke my heart, and it sent Joseph into the arms of another woman.

I know what heartbreak is.

I know that sacrifice.

I know the emptiness that follows.

I. Know.

Ten

Samantha

"HEY, SAM," MICHAEL GREETS ME AS I STEP OFF the elevator, having just gotten to Fin's from school.

"Hey." I walk through the front door, setting down my pack and purse. "I thought I wasn't going to see you today."

"Yeah, plans changed. When do you leave to see your mom?"

I plop on the couch, less than enthused by that prospect. My last visit, she cried the entire time. Fiona, Joseph's mom, says she really is making progress, but believes seeing me reminds my mom how much things have changed and how far she's slipped away from the life she used to have. She's at least started seeing someone to help her work through her grief, both one-on-one and in a group setting. But the idea of seeing her tonight...I'd rather not.

"About that. I don't think I'm gonna go. It only upsets her, and I end up feeling like crap afterwards." I glance up at him. "What's the point? She could care less if she sees me." She and Jace have written me off. I can only assume they blame me for my father's death, and they may be right. If I hadn't been there, the killer wouldn't have been able to use me as a pawn against Dad.

The cushion dips as Michael takes a seat next to me. "I could see how you'd feel that way. Give it more time, but don't think she doesn't care. I actually think she cares too much, and that's why it hurts so badly."

His normally closed-off eyes are warm and comforting. "I'm not making excuses for her. She's been a shit mom since your dad died. She's having a hard time coping, and that's her weakness, not yours. You haven't done anything wrong to warrant her treatment of you, or her lack of effort to make things better."

He takes my hand and holds it between his large, callused ones, turning it over, examining it. "You never know what you're made of until the shit hits the fan, then you truly know if you're made from strong stock or not."

His eyes narrow as he focuses on me. "You. You're made from some strong stock. Your mom and Jace, not so much, unfortunately. I still have hope for them, but you and I both know Jace was a mess even before all this stuff with your dad and you getting shot. I think it pushed him over the edge to crazy-whoring-town, and he can't seem to find his way back." He places my hand back on my lap. "He's always been a self-absorbed asshole who thought with his dick instead of his brain most times." He gets up and paces to the window. "I'm sorry. I really am. You deserve better."

I manage to hold in my bitter laugh. I probably deserve exactly what I've gotten. I won't debate it with Michael. There's no point. He would never agree with me, even if a part of him believed it to be true.

"We need to talk about the investigation." He turns, his face in shadow with the sunlight behind his back.

I squint to see his face, but it's no use. "Tell me."

"I wasn't at liberty to tell you these things before." He moves to the nearest chair, getting comfortable before he speaks again. "Your father worked with the FBI for many years. I only became aware of him in the last few years. By then, I had already met Jace through Fin and Joseph, so I pretty much had a conflict from the get-go with your father. However, my director believed I could keep my personal connection to Jace separate from my work with Daniel...your dad."

"You...you knew my dad? You actually worked with him? What was he?" I clasp my knees as I sit forward on the couch. "There's no way he was a spy. What did he do, perform surgeries on injured agents?"

"You're right. He wasn't a spy. It was his medical skills that interested the FBI." He moves to the edge of his seat, leaning closer, speaking softly. "And maybe other branches of the government too. I can't confirm, it's just a gut feeling."

My shock continues as Michael fills me in on the history of my dad's involvement with the FBI. Apparently, he came to their attention after his impressive work with the military in helping soldiers injured in service to their country. He performed procedures ranging from simple skin grafts to complete facial reconstruction. The latter was of primary interest to the FBI, where my father performed complete identity-changing facial reconstruction surgeries, allowing the patients to arrive pre-surgery looking like themselves, and leave looking like somebody completely different.

"Who were these people receiving new faces? Were they criminals? People in witness protection?"

"Majority of the time, it was agents, those you might consider spies, who needed to get lost, disappear, either for a job, or after a life-changing assignment forcing their retirement. I'm not going to lie to you and say some of your father's patients weren't unsavory, but he was not allowed to know their names, their circumstances, or why they were having surgery. He only knew what was pertinent for his job, which was all medical-related. Everything else was on a need-to-know basis, and your father did not need to know those facts to perform his job, nor was it safe for him to know those details. He trusted his government was making the right call. He felt he was being called to service his country by using the gifts he had."

Michael's hand encapsulates mine and squeezes. "He helped so many military men and woman have better lives because of his surgical skills, including his regular patients. Your father never took a frivolous job for vanity's sake. He could have made a killing as a Hollywood plastic surgeon, catering to the wealthy who sought and paid premium dollar for bigger boobs, smaller noses, and skinnier waistlines. But he didn't. He had a higher calling to fix what was broken either by birth, chance, or war."

I swipe at a tear. "You make him sound like a saint, Michael."

He gifts me with a rare smile. "To his patients, he was a saint, a godsend. To the government, he was a highly sought-after practitioner of healing what many thought could not be fixed, including the occasional identity-changing surgery. He didn't do many, only a few a year. His main involvement, his true gift, was simply fixing what had been broken by circumstance or fate."

I collapse back into the couch, closing my eyes, trying to comprehend the depth of my father's skills and the number of lives he impacted in a positive way. It makes me proud. It also makes me terribly sad that he never got to share this amazing part of himself with us. He was a hero, a bigger hero than any of his family knew. He'll no longer be able to help anyone ever again.

I slowly open my eyes to the reality of this conversation. "Why are you telling me this? What does it all have to do with his death?"

After another slight smile and knowing nod, I think I passed some secret test. "I'm glad you see the correlation, Sam. I want you to remember all the positive things he did as we talk about the man who brought death and mayhem to your door."

Joseph

I miss my girl. It's hard not to fly home every weekend, not to spend every night with her safely tucked in my arms. I want to. Christ, I want it more than I need to draw my next breath. But I promised her I'd stay away, for a few weeks at least.

I'm on a countdown. She graduates next month, and come hell or high water, I'm going to be there. I don't give a flying fuck what Fin, Michael, or Victor think about it. *I'm going.* There's no way I'd miss my girl graduating and giving her valedictorian speech.

The only positive thing about me staying away is it gives her the space she needs to come to terms with what's happening between us. Not that she has any choice in the matter. I have no intentions of letting her go. I don't want to steamroll her, though. She needs time to absorb it, live with the idea, let it ruminate without me hovering over her, breathing down her neck both figuratively and literally. If I were there, there would be no break from my physical need to be near her, touch her, woo her, love her, and most definitely protect her.

If it were up to me, we'd be living in our own fortress by now where no one would ever get inside to hurt or scare her again. But that's not a life. That's a prison.

Victor is still watching her, which has become much easier with her living at Fin's. Michael is as communicative as he can be without putting his job in jeopardy. He's already broken too many rules by coming to see me after Samantha broke up with me. He knew something was wrong as soon as she didn't go to work for two days and didn't get out of bed until he made her get up the following day. It took my remorse to a whole new level to hear she'd taken to her bed and didn't get up for two days after she broke up with me and after the news of me cheating on her, so she thinks. I understand that level of devastation and sorrow. I felt it too, deeply, inexcusably.

And being apart from her now is even worse when I know she's in danger.

Sometimes life gives you just what you need when you need it. So when her face pops up on my phone, a warmth floods my chest, and I feel forgiven, though we still have obstacles to traverse. The truth. Will she ever know the truth?

"Samantha, baby."

"Joseph."

The sadness in her voice sets me on edge. "What's wrong?"

She takes a deep breath, and it seems like an eternity before she speaks again. "I just...needed to hear your voice. I miss you. I know you're staying away because I asked you to, but I wish you were here. I just want to feel your arms wrapped around me, telling me everything's going to be alright."

If she asked, I would drop everything and fly, drive, walk, and even crawl to my girl. "Sweetness, I miss you too. You're making it hard for me to stay away. Tell me what happened. Aren't you seeing your mom tonight?"

"I canceled. I couldn't take another visit, feeling like it doesn't matter if I'm dead or alive. So, I copped out. I didn't even have the guts to do it myself. Michael called your mom for me. I don't know what he'll tell her, but I doubt it'll be the truth."

"Don't feel bad about it. Sometimes you have to put yourself first—and you rarely do so. Take a few weeks and see how you feel. But, Samantha, your mom cares you're alive. It does matter to her, even if she's doing a piss poor job of showing you. I'm not defending her. No one is under the illusion that how she and Jace have pulled away from you is okay. It's not. I think you stepping back is completely understandable. Maybe you should stop trying. Let her be the one to reach out to you."

She lets out a long sigh. "Thank you for your support. I think you're right. It only hurts me and makes me mad every time I open up to her and try to be there for her. I'm so tired of trying to make it better, make *her* better. If she was making an effort, it would be different. But she's not, so I'm done, at least for now."

"I don't know if you need to hear it or not, but I, for one, am damn happy you're alive, Samantha. And anyone who doesn't relish that fact doesn't deserve to be in your life. Step away for a while. Let me handle it. I'll talk to my parents. I think it's time to put her in a facility where they can take care of her 24/7, give her the psychological help she requires. It might be the wake-up call—or boost—she needs." I make a mental note to call my dad as soon as we hang up.

"God, I feel nearly as guilty as I feel relieved. I should be the one to handle it, but I can't, or don't want to. I'm not entirely sure which, to be honest."

"No guilt. I've got this. It's my honor to do this for you. Anything. Anytime. Always."

"Thank you."

"No thanks needed, but you're welcome all the same." I settle back on my bed. "Now, tell me what happened today. What's going on?"

My sweet girl fills me in on her conversation with Michael and the details behind her dad's murder. Michael didn't give her any names, rightly so. It would only put her in more danger.

"That's some crazy shit. So, your dad performed facial reconstruction surgery on a guy your dad's killer has been trying to find for years, and he thought your dad had information about the guy's new identity?"

"Yep. It makes sense. That day in the parking lot, he told my dad to go to his office and get the information he wanted, while he kept me as collateral."

"The idea of you being held at gunpoint, Samantha. I...want to kill him. For scaring you, for taking your father from you, for shooting you. If I ever see him, I won't hesitate. Not for a goddamn second." My blood boils at the thought of him hurting my girl, using her to get what he wants.

She surprises me by laughing. "Sometimes, I really love the caveman in you."

Love. Christ, please say those three little words to me.

"Yeah?" I say, instead of what's in my heart. She's not ready to hear me say those three all-important words. She's opening up to me more and more each day, learning to trust that I'm not going anywhere, that she can count on me. I'm not like Jace—dumping her at every turn, and I pray I'm not leaving her like her father did. I don't want to scare her off, shut her down by saying them too soon. Too soon by her standards.

"It's hot."

Aaaaaand my dick is hard.

"Samantha." I don't even try to hide my growl.

"See, just like that. It's hot as hell, Joseph. It makes me feel cherished, special."

Jesus. And just like that it goes from sexual to intimate. "Sweetness, you are special and beyond cherished." I need to see her. I need to hold my girl.

"Keep talking to me, Joseph. I need to hear your voice."

Anything for my girl.

Anywhere.

Anytime.

Always.

Eleven

Samantha

MY HEART IS GONNA BEAT OUT OF MY CHEST. *HOLY crap!*

But wait. What if it's nothing?

What if it's something?

Shit!

"What was that, Sam?" Victor looks at me in the rearview mirror, his eyes hidden by his sunglasses, jaw tight. His demeanor gives away nothing, as usual.

Did I say something? "Uh, is Michael around? Do you know?"

He glances at Smith, Michael's man, my bodyguard for the day, sitting in the passenger seat. I'm pretty sure *Smith* is not his real name. He shrugs.

Victor's attention is back on me. "I'm not sure, but I can find out."

My knee bounces in rhythm with my heart. I don't want to make a big deal of this. "It's okay. I was just wondering."

I focus out the window, but I can still feel Victor's eyes on me. "You sure?" he presses.

"Yeah." *Is he buying my nonchalance?*

I'm lost in thought when the car comes to a halt, and I'm confused as to why we're not in the garage of MCI towers. "What are we doing?"

Victor frowns and motions to the building to my right. "It's Thursday. You have physical therapy today."

Oh shit! I totally forgot. Maybe it will be good to work off some of this nervous energy.

I glance at my backpack and back at him. "Are you waiting? Should I take my stuff with me?"

He turns around, gauging me. "What's going on, Sam? I can smell your nerves from here."

What the fuck? "Are you saying I stink?"

He laughs. "No! I'm saying you're nervous as fuck, and if I were a predator, I could smell your fear. Now, what's going on?"

"Nothing." I open my door and hop out before he can stop me or question me further.

Smith is at my side with my gym bag in hand. I glance back at the car and the back door where my backpack sits on the floorboard along with my purse and cell phone. I want to go back and get them, but Victor will be more suspicious than ever since I usually leave them in the car during therapy. I glance at the front seat where Victor's removed his shades and is eyeballing me with a fearsome gaze.

Shit. Why do I think I can hide anything from him?

Smith's hand on my shoulder stops me from smacking into the glass door. I kept walking, even though my attention was on the car and not where I was going.

Cool move, dipshit. I have to get a grip on my nerves.

I enter through the double doors fully expecting Victor to follow and start interrogating me. Thankfully, after I've changed into my work-out clothes, he's nowhere to be seen. I relax. Maybe, just maybe, I got away with my evasiveness.

Agent Smith assumes his pillar impression against the nearest wall, close but not so close that he'll be a hindrance to my therapy.

I'm always surprised when no one asks me about the security following me around. I've started to think Michael, Victor, or maybe even Joseph calls ahead to warn people, asking them not to acknowledge or mention them to me. Even at school, rarely does anyone say anything to me about my stream of larger-than-your-average-guy protection following me around everywhere I go. I do mean everywhere. The first few days, they cleared the restroom before I entered to be sure it was safe. It only took a few screaming female students for the principal to grant me access to the teachers' restricted bathrooms. Their one-occupant facilities allow my protection to open the door, scan the room, and then stand outside while I do my business like a dog on a leash. I'm not complaining, not really. It's just an interesting position to be in and see how people react to them, or in this case, do not react to them.

My hour therapy session is over before I realize, and I'm more than happy to be heading home. I've got less than a month of school left and lots of projects to wrap up before graduation. Though, tonight I'm going to be sidetracked with the envelope in my bag.

Victor doesn't say anything to me on the ride home other than to ask how my therapy went. Once in the garage and escorted to the elevator, I'm allowed to ride up by myself, which is unusual. Normally, Michael or one of the other guys escorts me. With the elevator key in place, it's an express ride to the penthouse floor, so it's not like I'm in danger from the garage to Fin's apartment. However, if I'm right about what I suspect is in my bag, I doubt even this small reprieve from security will be allowed again.

As the elevator slows, so do my thoughts and my rush to get inside to find the answers I seek. The doors open, and I step out slowly, debating about heading up to the pool level for a moment of true peaceful solitude.

Yes. That's what I'll do. The envelope's not going anywhere.

I turn toward the rooftop stairwell.

With a click of a door down the hall, my heart jumps into overdrive as thoughts of my father's killer cloud my vision. Someone's here.

Without even a moment's hesitation, I take off for the stairs, and as I breach the doorway, I realize my fatal flaw.

Where will I go once I'm on the roof? Jump? Not likely. There's nowhere to go.

Sweat beads on my forehead.

Damn! What the fuck am I going to do now?

A strong hand lands on my left shoulder, stopping me in my tracks.

I grip that hand, bending the thumb back, and I spin around to face my attacker.

"Sam!"

"Jesus, fuck, Michael!" I step back and release him, but not before noting the pain on his face. *Shit.*

"Sam, what the fuck?" He's not angry like I expect, which throws me off even more. I move back, stumbling on the first step.

He's there, lightning fast, pulling me upright before I hit any hard surface of the stairs or wall, and instead crash into him, a solid wall of muscle.

"Breathe, Sam. What the fuck's going on?"

I cling to him, my knees weak and my head spinning. "I…you… scared me."

He scoops me in his arms and storms out of the stairwell, rounds the corner, and heads into Fin's apartment.

I don't struggle. I can't get my bearings. I can't even get enough air.

He sits me on the couch, pushing my head forward. "Put your head between your knees. That's it. Breathe, princess."

"Michael—"

"Shh. Just breathe. Give yourself a moment to calm down." He pats my back. "Stay here. I'm going to go get your stuff. You dropped it in the stairwell."

His voice trails from behind me as he heads out the door. "Better?" He kneels beside me a moment later, holding out a glass of water.

I push back into the couch and try to take the glass from him, but my hand shakes.

His hand clasps over mine, helping me take a drink. "It's the adrenaline. Take another sip, finish it if you can." As I drink, he scans my face. "You're still white as a ghost. You sure you're okay?"

I finish off the water, and he sets the glass on the coffee table before I can answer him. "Yeah."

He settles in the chair next to me. "Good job on taking me down, by the way."

I roll my eyes. "I didn't come anywhere close to taking you down."

"You would have if you hadn't pulled back as soon as you realized it was me. I was on my way to my knees with the vise-like grip you had on my thumb and arm." He nods. "It was quick thinking. You did good."

"No. It wasn't." I move to the end of the couch, slipping off my shoes and curling my feet under me. I search for the blanket that's usually behind the couch.

"Here." Michael tosses me the blanket. "Cold?"

I wrap it around me, pulling it up under my chin. "Yes."

"That's to be expected too."

Great. Shaky. Cold. And Emotional. Fun times.

I return to his comment from a moment ago. "I shouldn't have gone to the stairwell, but it was too late by the time I realized my mistake. I should have gotten back in the elevator."

He shakes his head. "The doors had already closed. You made the right move for where you were and for where I was. It was good self-defense even if you don't feel like it was. You had limited options, and your instincts chose correctly."

I guess I'll take that. He is the expert, after all.

"Why were you loitering out in the hall, anyway? And what happened today?" He points at me. "And don't even think of trying to blow me off like you did Victor. He knew something was up, but he didn't want to push you. He called me, and I came straight here, waiting on you to get home."

"I was thinking of going up to the pool and taking a swim."

He frowns not liking that idea. "What happened at school?"

"Where's my backpack?"

"I'll get it." He heads to the entryway. "Victor said you were weird about leaving your stuff in the car during therapy. I can only assume there's something in there you need to show me, and that's why you were asking for me."

He sets my pack down next to me. "You could have called me, you know."

I unzip my pack but don't touch it. I glance up at him. "I didn't want to bother you. Especially if it's nothing."

He sits on the coffee table in front of me. "Sam, you're upset. Something got under your skin today, enough to spook you, make you nervous, secretive, and paranoid. When you stepped off the elevator and heard the door open, you feared for your life. Did it feel like nothing?"

"No." I crack. "It felt like the farthest away from nothing it possibly could be."

"Exactly." He brushes a tear from my cheek. "Next time, call me, even if it's during school. Even if you know I've got something important going on, you can still call me. If I can't answer, one of my guys will call you right back. But you could've called Victor or talked to him in the car. You didn't need to carry this fear around all day, letting it grow and fester. It may have started out as nothing, but it most definitely is not nothing now." He glances at my backpack and then back at me.

"It's an envelope. It's addressed to me. It was sitting on my desk in my macroeconomics class when I arrived." I hold open my bag so he can see inside. "I didn't open it. There was something about it, setting off red flags. I only touched the right-hand corner getting it into my pack."

He leans forward, straining to see the envelope without touching it. "Stay here." He takes my pack to the kitchen.

I don't argue with him. This is his area of expertise, and whether I see what's in the envelope first or last, he's still going to see it, so there's no point in making a fuss. Besides, I'm actually relieved to no longer be responsible for it being in my possession.

I hear him talking on the phone. I can't make anything out, only the murmur of his voice. A few minutes later my phone rings just as Victor walks in the front door, nods at me, and heads to the kitchen.

I round the couch to get my phone from my purse, eyeing the kitchen to see what they're doing in there. "Hello?"

"Did you get my letter?"

My vision narrows, and a scream rips from me as I drop my phone. That voice. I'll never forget that voice. Not as long as I live will I forget that accent I can't place, or the steely calm of his overly pronounced words.

My knees buckle, and somehow Michael catches me in a huff as my dead weight takes us both to the floor.

"It was him." I gasp. "He wanted to know if I got his letter."

PART 5
HIGHS AND LOWS

Twelve

Joseph

AFTER AN URGENT CALL FROM VICTOR, I HOPPED on the first flight I could get and flew home. It's been two days since I've spoken to my girl. We've texted. Lots. But no phone calls. I miss her voice. I called her earlier today, but she didn't answer. Now I know why.

One of Victor's men picked me up from the airport, so I'll have to wait to get any further details once I'm at the penthouse. Samantha will probably already be asleep when I get there. It won't stop me from going to her as soon as I'm done talking to Michael and Victor.

We pull into the underground garage, and I hop out barely before the car is in park. My bag in hand, I head toward the elevator. I'm a man on a mission, no time for bullshit.

I open the door to Fin's penthouse. It's late and quiet, except for the low murmur of voices I hear in the distance. The lights are dim, giving the illusion of calm, but there's nothing calm about what went down here today. I find Fin, Michael, and Victor in Fin's office.

"She'll be happy to see you," Fin says, not even looking up from his desk.

"Probably not as happy as I'll be to see her." I acknowledge Victor and Michael. "Is she sleeping?"

Michael surprises me with a hug and a smile. He must be drunk. "She should be. I put her to bed over an hour ago."

I stop in my tracks. "What do you mean you *'put her to bed?'*"

Fin finally lifts his head. "Calm, caveman. He was just looking out for her."

"I trust Michael, bro. I'm more concerned that she needed assistance. Is she okay?"

"She's fine, just tired is all," Michael assures me.

Fin leans back in his chair and motions to the bar. "Do you want a drink?"

I set my bag down. "Just some water. Do you want anything?"

Fin holds up his tumbler of amber liquid and turns back to his computer. "I'm good."

Michael and Victor indicate they're fine too.

I put ice in a glass and grab a bottled water. I plant myself in the closest wingback chair, allowing me to see all three of them. Fin glances up from his computer when he hears the ice crackle as I pour water into my glass.

"Will you be working very late?" I ask Fin, wondering how many nights he stays up late in his office.

"Not very. I left a little early tonight because of the situation here, so I have a few things to finish up before calling it a day," he says, then takes a slow sip of his Macallan scotch.

I'm not much of a whiskey man, but I could grow to love my brother's stockpile of vintage 1939 Macallan. It has a sweet toffee undertone that's hard to resist.

"So. Fill me in, Michael. From the beginning." I'm anxious to get to Samantha, but I need to hear this to help me gauge her state of mind.

Michael finishes off his whiskey with a deep sigh. I can almost feel the sweet burn he must be experiencing. He nods to Victor. "He noticed Sam acting nervous and distracted as soon as he picked her and Agent Smith up from school."

"She was a bundle of nerves, but downplayed it without much success," Victor adds.

"Well, she couldn't have been too much of a basket case or Smith would have noticed. Or he *should* have noticed," I point out. Smith needs to move on to another assignment.

"Agreed." The censure in Michael eyes conveys he's on the same page about Smith.

The two of them fill me in, with the majority of the details coming from Michael.

"Fuck, she thought you were the killer?" I stop Michael as he gets to the part in the stairwell.

"Yeah, by that point her nerves where so amped up, and she didn't have protection in the elevator, her imagination got the best of her. Plus, she wasn't aware of me waiting for her. We thought it best not to tell her, so she didn't have time to come up with an excuse not to tell us what's going on. In hindsight, probably not the best move on our part. On a positive note, she responded to the perceived threat like a champ. I'm proud of her."

That is something to be thankful for. I let him continue retelling the events as they unfolded. My gut clenches when I hear about her reaction to the killer's phone call. I can barely stand another minute before going to her.

"Can I see the letter?" I debate getting a glass of whiskey, but I need to stay sober and strong for Samantha. I don't need my senses dulled by alcohol.

"The original has already been sent for forensics analysis, but we have a copy." Michael grabs a piece of paper off Fin's desk and hands it over.

I take a moment to read through it once, then again.

Sam,

I can't express to you how sorry I am for what happen in the parking lot that day. I had no intention of shoot you or your father. It was just a convincing threat to get what I needed from him. You can still help me. You can make all of this go way. You can make me go way by helping me get what I need. No one else need get hurt.

I'm reasonable man. I know I hurt you deeply. I don't expect you to forgive me, but I am sorry. Please, help me make right a wrong done to me by help me get the information I seek. It's not too late. Then, I promise to disappear. You will never hear from me again.

Rod

"Rod?"

"His name is Roderick Hoffman. He's German," Michael advises.

"German? Huh. Samantha said she couldn't place the accent, familiar, yet not."

"That's because he's German but was raised by his mother in Johannesburg until his teens. His accent is a combination of the two, according to our intel." Michael looks at all three of us, pointing to the letter. "This is good news. We've needed a break in the case. Him reaching out to her means he's desperate. He's also putting himself out there, which makes it easier for us to catch him. But mainly, it means we have a way to get to him, to set him up."

I set the letter back on the desk. "You mean to use Samantha as bait."

"We're throwing around ideas." Michael moves closer. "She's the only connection we have to him. He reached out to her in the letter and the phone call. He used a burner cell. He could have called from a public phone, but instead he left a way for her to contact him. We mean to take full advantage." He runs his fingers through his hair and pops his neck. "I won't pretend it's not dangerous for her." He and Victor exchange glances. "We're working on a secondary plan as well, one that does not involve the FBI. It's another layer of protection. She won't go out there unprotected or unarmed."

"Unarmed? You plan to arm her? Christ." I pace to the window.

Fin stands to refill his drink. "It's a precautionary measure. A third redundancy, if you will. Victor and Michael have been working on her fighting skills, and, as she proved tonight, she's a quick study. She's Texas born and raised, no stranger to firearms. Daniel made sure both his kids knew how to shoot. Victor's guys will work with Sam on brushing up her skills." He nods to Michael. "Michael will be out of the loop. Plausible deniability since Sam carrying a gun is not a government-sanctioned practice."

Christ almighty. "When?"

Victor stands and joins us in the middle of the room. "We're thinking her graduation ceremony. She can convince Roderick it's the best choice because of the amount of people in attendance. She'll tell him she's under surveillance 24/7, but certain she can slip away in the midst of all those people. From our side, the crowd gives us better cover and allows us to bring in more manpower. She'll also have trackers on her, some of them FBI trackers and some of them ours. They'll be on her body and hidden in her belongings/clothing."

"What if he searches her?" I interject.

"We'll have a few in obvious places we're sure he'll find. It's normal protocol for a subject to have trackers and not know it. Sam won't be aware of where they are, so she'll have plausible deniability." Victor's confidence in this plan is comforting.

"You already have trackers on her, don't you?" I glance between Michael and Victor. They simply nod in confirmation. Figures.

Fin, ever the peacekeeper, suggests we let it rest for tonight. "Come on, caveman. I'll walk you to her room. I assume you're staying with her?"

"Yep." I've never been awkward about being with a woman before, but admitting I'm planning on sleeping with Samantha seems different. Not wrong, just more intimate, and not something I want to share with anyone, even Fin. Talking about it feels like I'm breaking a sacred trust.

"Do you need anything? Protection?" He almost seems embarrassed to ask.

I stop in my tracks. "Fin, I'm not having sex with her."

He scoffs. "Well, in case you change your mind, there's a box on condoms and some other stuff in the other guest bath. I didn't think she'd appreciate me putting them in her room."

"Jesus, Fin, you bought condoms for us? I'm not sixteen. I know how to have safe sex." I should probably be mad, but I'm actually finding it quite humorous.

He shrugs, seemingly uncomfortable. "I know. I know. I just… well…fuck. It's Sam. I just wanted to be sure you were safe. Prepared."

"She's gotten to you, hasn't she? She hasn't just been working on Victor and Michael. She's been working on you too."

"Joe, it's not like that. I feel protective of her. I care for her. I've been watching over her while you and Jace have been away. I'm like her surrogate parent, her adopted brother, and her friend, all rolled into one."

I back down. "I'm not accusing you of anything. I'm just jealous you've gotten to spend all this time with her. She seems to really respond to you, to like you. I, on the other hand, haven't spoken to her in two days, and I'm worried she won't be happy to see me."

He squeezes my shoulder. "Joe, she's scared. She's worried you're gonna find someone older, more experienced, more of what she thinks you need in a life partner. She's lost so much. She's afraid of losing you either to your career path or the killer. She needs reassurance she's the one, and that both of you are safe."

"That's shit, Fin. I couldn't find anyone better than her. Ever. I could scan the globe for the rest of my life and not find anyone half as amazing as she is."

"You don't have to convince me. You have to convince her."

I sigh, rubbing my hand across my face. "I know."

"So why are you still standing here with me?"

"Fuck. Alright, I'm going."

He stops me before I open the door. "Oh, I got her out of school tomorrow. You're welcome." He laughs as he disappears down the hall.

Fucker.

Thirteen

Joseph

GET READY FOR BED IN THE GUEST ROOM ACROSS the hall so as not to wake her. Well, not to wake her until I'm ready to wake her. Since she doesn't have to get up in the morning, I'm most definitely waking her up. I need to see her, to touch her, to lose myself in her scent, to connect with her in a more tangible way than text messages. But, mostly I need to be sure she's okay after the events of today.

I set my phone on the nightstand and hit play. The volume is low, and it only takes a moment for my love song to her, *I Get to Love You*, to fill the stillness of her room.

She doesn't stir until I climb in bed behind her, blanketing her body with mine, and whisper ever so softly against her ear, "Sweetness."

"Hmmm," she responds, pressing her body into mine, still asleep, but knowing I'm here, at least on some level.

I cradle her with my body, her back to my front. She's so warm, tucked in under the covers, it's like rubbing up against warm silk. I bury my nose in her hair. "Christ, you smell good." I run my nose along the curve of her neck and kiss up her shoulder. "Like spring flowers and you."

"Joseph, you're here," she murmurs, reaching her arm up, stretching, and rolling slightly onto her stomach.

I roll with her, pressing into her back, not letting any distance come between us. "Of course, I'm here." I wrap my arms around her. "Tell me you're okay, Sweetness."

"I was so scared." Her soft, hoarse words shoot straight to my heart. It pains me I wasn't here for her, but then she rubs her face against my cheek. "I'm okay, Joseph. And you're here. You came."

I unfurl from around her and move so she can see my face. "Always. I will always come for you."

She sighs and gives me a sweet smile, soothing me. I kiss along her back as my hand caresses up her outstretched arm, entwining our fingers, and press into her, swiveling my hips.

"Joseph," she gasps as her body moves with mine.

"I love to hear my name on your lips." I move lower, rubbing my face, my lips, my hand down her back until I reach the bottom of her camisole. I slowly start to work it up her body, kissing and caressing as her bare skin is revealed. Her skin is so soft, every inch of her perfection. When I've lifted her cami as far as I can, she rocks gently, allowing me to pull it off over her head.

She tries to roll over, but I stop her. As much as I want to be bare chest to bare chest, I'm not done exploring her back. I start at her head, losing my fingers in her mane of brownish red locks, sweeping the silkiness aside. My mouth settles on her neck, kissing behind her ear, nipping and then licking her earlobe. She squirms, mumbling like she meant to say my name, but she wasn't quite capable.

It makes me smile. She's still trying to wake up, and I'm inundating her with my body, full force, not giving her a chance to settle and get used to my presence.

I kiss down her back and relish every squirm, sigh, and moan. "You're so beautiful, Samantha." I nip at her side. "Tell me how you can ever allow anyone to call you Sam?"

"Joseph, please," she whispers.

"Please what?" I stop my journey southward and return to hover near her head, needing to hear what she is pleading for.

"I don't want to talk about that." Her voice is sexy and seductive, and she doesn't have a clue how it affects me.

"What do you want then?" I probe.

"You. I just want you," she says.

My lips return to her shoulder, kissing along her arm and then back to her neck as I reply, "And I you, baby. Tell me what you don't want to say. I need to understand, as I don't see how someone as gorgeous as you can be called by anything other than Samantha, goddess of my heart."

"Joseph." It's a plea, of what, I'm not sure. Maybe it's for me to continue my exploration of her body, or for me to stop this line of questioning. Perhaps it's both.

"Tell me, and I'll give you anything you want." I'll give her anything she wants anyway.

She buries her head in her pillow and turns the other way, trying to hide. "When you hear the name *Sam*, what do you think of? Who do you picture?"

"That's easy." I shrug and move so I can see her face over her other shoulder, my body still covering hers, straddling her hips, my hard cock pressed against her ass. "I picture some guy, non-descript, but definitely a guy."

She nods. "And what do you picture when you hear the name Samantha?"

I smile. "That's even easier. I picture you, Sweetness."

She shakes her head. "Nope. Before me, before you even knew I existed."

"I guess I pictured a woman. A woman with silken hair, curvaceous curves, graceful and seductive. Beautiful."

"Exactly," is all she says, not a word more.

I don't understand. I rise up and roll her over. "Exactly what?"

She sighs in exasperation. "If I meet you for the first time and you're expecting a Sam, then in most cases you'll be pleasantly surprised to see me. But, if you're expecting a Samantha, I can't live up to the ideals men conjure in their heads." She brushes her hand across my forehead. "As Sam, I rise above the curve. As Samantha, I fall below."

"Christ, is that what you think?"

"It's what I know to be true." She sounds so sure. She truly believes that crap.

"Either you're hanging out with idiots, or someone's sold you a load of crap. Who put this idea in your head? Who made you feel you didn't live up to your name?"

She shakes her head. "It doesn't matter. It's true. Sam fits me better. No one calls me Samantha except you. Not even my parents, who named me, actually ever called me by it. That means something."

She moves to get up, but I stop her from pulling away. She falls back, locking eyes with me. "Everyone calls you Joe. Why is Joe good enough for you, but Sam isn't good enough for me?"

Capturing her hands beside her head, our fingers lock in an embrace. "Only you and my grandmother call me Joseph. As for everyone else, you're right, they call me Joe."

I kiss across her cheek and stop at her lips. "It's different, though. I don't insist people call me Joe because I don't feel worthy of Joseph. I couldn't give a fuck if they call me Joe or Joseph, it doesn't change my opinion of myself." I run my nose along hers. "Except you. I like it when you call me Joseph because it seems special, to hold more meaning." I press my lips to hers in a slow, tender kiss. Pulling away momentarily, I study her face. "Tell me who hurt you, Samantha. Who boxed you in, keeping you hostage to a boy's name?"

"I like you calling me Samantha. It irritated me at first, but then I understood you weren't making fun of me. It meant something to you. It's special when you say it, and now I don't want anyone else to call me Samantha. Only you."

"It is special." I kiss her, capturing her bottom lip, pulling slightly. "Now stop trying to distract me. Tell me who hurt you?" I'm not giving up, I'm like a dog with a bone, and this bone needs to be buried.

Even in the dim light I can see her studying me, contemplating her next move. "Jace," she says so softly, I would have missed it had I not seen her lips move.

What the fuck? Jace, man. Christ.

I roll onto my back and pull her into my arms. "What'd he say, Sweetness?"

"We were young, Joseph. Don't be mad at him. He has no idea what he said made a lasting impression."

"Samantha." I'm losing my patience, not with her, with Jace. He's impacted her so much, and he has no idea. Now I have to hear how he's stifled her opinion of herself with her name on top of the fact he already made her feel unwanted when no one would date her due to him putting out a moratorium on her.

"Okay. Okay. I was twelve or so. I got a wild hair and starting asking everyone to call me Samantha. I thought it sounded more glamorous, more grown up. But when Jace heard me tell someone my name was Samantha, he started laughing and said, '*Sam, you're too much of a tomboy to ever be called Samantha. Those are shoes you'll never fill.*' So, I dropped it and went back to being Sam. I've been Sam ever since."

Christ, he's a fucking idiot. He and I are going to have words. Again. I nudge her. "Samantha, look at me."

She props up, her chin resting on her hands splayed across my chest.

"We've already established your brother's an idiot on a good day. I have no doubt, if he thought you would take what he said to heart, he never would have said it. He was being flippant and irresponsible, and a kid. He was only what, fourteen? He didn't know jack-shit about life." I cup her face. "You more than surpass your name in beauty and intellect. Maybe you were a tomboy and Sam seemed to fit when you were a kid, but you're all woman now, and *Samantha* you will always be to me. If you continue to request people call you Sam, do so because you only want *me* to call you *Samantha*, and not because you feel unworthy of such a name."

I roll over, pressing into her, only this time we are chest to chest. I cup her face, running my thumb down the line of her cheekbone. "Samantha, you are the most beautiful woman I have ever seen. From the moment I saw you, you captured my mind, my body, and my heart. You are a goddess. You are my goddess. My *Samantha*. Tell me *my* words carry as much weight as Jace's words did when you were just twelve. Tell me your mature eighteen-year-old ears hear me now, beautiful."

Her eyes continue to study mine. Her hands travel to my

shoulders, holding me close. "I want to be what you see, Joseph. I want to be your *Samantha.*"

"There's no *want*, Sweetness. You *are.*" I lower my head, brushing my lips across hers. "Let me love you. Let me show you what you mean to me." I tear my gaze from hers and move down to her breasts, smiling up at her. "I'm going to get lost in these beauties." I settle lower, between her thighs, her glorious breasts staring back at me. "Anything you don't want me to do, just say so. I'm not rushing this. We're not having sex, but I'm going to explore every inch of you, Samantha. Every inch of you is going to be mine by the time I'm done."

She arches, wiggling below me. "Joseph."

"Christ, I love how you say my name when you're all hot and bothered. Don't hold back, baby. Don't ever hold back. I always want to hear how much I please you." With that, I'm done talking, done analyzing anything except how to read her body, how to make her feel good. I capture her taut nipple in my mouth, sucking deeply. My hand continues to tease the other one, pinching and pulling gently.

She nearly bows off the bed. "Oh, god."

I lose myself in the clasp of her arms holding me in place, her round breasts to sink my face into, and hard, sensitive nipples beckoning for my mouth to suck and lick. I'm so turned on, my cock aches for relief, but I don't care. This is all about her, and I'm in the haze of her arousal, pulling me to her, begging for more.

She clasps my face, forcing me to release her. She's breathless and has a pained expression.

Pained? Shit, have I been so wrapped up in her body I didn't notice I was hurting her?

"Joseph, please," she pleads.

I move up her body. "Christ, have I hurt you? What's wrong?" I scan her face, her breasts, and run my hand over her injured shoulder for signs of trauma.

She cups my cheek, bringing my face back to hers. She's still panting, crazed, maybe confused. "I ache, Joseph. I can't take any more."

Realization dawns. "Sweetness, you need release." My hand travels down her body and slips inside her panties. She's soaked. "Fuck, baby." I sink my fingers between her folds and back up to her clit. "Kiss me. Show me what you need."

She lunges and nearly knocks me back. I quickly recover my position over her. Her tongue flicks across mine as my finger circles her clit. She moans and sucks my tongue. My cock twitches, eager with the idea of her sucking on it.

Christ, I'm gonna come in my underwear if I keep thinking like that.

I adjust, lying half on her, using my leg to open her thighs to me more. I sink my tongue in past her lips, making love to her mouth as I wish my cock could do to her pussy. She cries out, her nails biting into my back, turning me on even more. Her hips undulate, teasing and begging for more, more of the things I can't give her. Not yet, anyway.

I pull on her bottom lip, releasing it as my fingers pinch her nipple, rolling it, teasing it along with her clit. "Come for me."

"Joseph," she cries out, arching back, legs shaking as her orgasm takes flight.

"So fucking beautiful. I can't wait to be buried inside you, feeling you come undone around my cock."

She lets out a long moan, and I almost come, knowing how my words affect her. I suck on her breasts as I continue to circle her clit, prolonging her orgasm, extracting every bit of her pleasure.

When she loosens her grip on my back and starts to relax, I trail kiss down her body. I'm on a mission of a different kind. The destination is the same, but the journey much different.

"Lift up." Without hesitation, she lifts her hips, allowing me to pull off her panties.

She's laid out, completely naked before me. "You're exquisite, Samantha. The most beautiful creature I've ever seen."

Her hand snakes in my hair. "What are you doing, Joseph?" Her face is languid, beautiful without a stitch of makeup on.

"Exploring." I run my nose along her closely cropped landing strip, guiding me to my destination. "You smell so good." I spread her legs, burrowing my shoulders under her knees.

"Joseph," she screeches. "I'm not sure..." Her words are lost as my tongue sweeps her folds. "Oh, god!"

"Christ, you taste even better than I imagined."

She jumps as I lick her clit.

"You'd better settle in, Sweetness, this is going to take a while. I imagine two to three orgasms, at least."

Samantha

"Joseph, I can't possibly. You don't need to do that. I just had a quite spectacular orgasm. I don't need more." I rise up on my elbows, gazing down at the most handsome man I've ever seen looking up at me from between my thighs.

My thighs! Never in my wildest dreams did I picture him there, like this. Well, I did picture him, but honestly, my imagination is poorly lacking, as the reality is so much sweeter.

He flashes a devious smile. "Sweetness, you have no idea what your body can do." His tongue licks across my opening, pushing, but not breaching my virgin passageway.

My insides clench, wanting him to enter me, wanting him to be the one to take my virginity, to claim me in all ways.

My head falls back. "Please."

"Please what?" His tongue does it again. "Do you want me inside you? Do you want me to fill you up, take your virginity, make you mine?" He echoes my thoughts.

I push up on my hands, my eyes finding his. "Don't fuck with me, Joseph."

He frowns. "You're right. I'm sorry. I'm teasing you, but I'm not trying to make light of the situation. I want to explore you, but I won't enter you. I won't take that precious gift. Don't get me wrong, Samantha. I will be your first and last lover, but we're in no hurry. I want to savor every inch of you, cherish everything you give me. I won't take your virginity until you're ready to be mine. Forever."

He rises to his hands and knees, climbing up my body to hover over me, forcing me to lie back down. His face is mere inches from mine. "In case you don't know it. I love you. I'm in love with you."

In love with me? *Oh, shit.* This man. He takes me places I feared to imagine but hoped were possible.

"I will kiss you. I will suck your nipples. I will touch you. I will eat your pussy and explore every inch of you, making you come in every way possible. But I won't take your virginity until you are ready to give yourself to me. Fully. Endlessly. Forever."

"Joseph, I'm willing to give you my virginity now. You don't have to wait." I touch his erection through his underwear. He hisses and closes his eyes. "Let me touch you and give you pleasure. It isn't just about me."

He bends down and kisses my neck and then bites me. I yelp, and he soothes it with his tongue. "Samantha, you can touch me, you can lick me, you can suck me, you can do anything you like to me, anytime you like. But, you still don't fully believe in our future. Together. You don't fully trust me not to leave you, abandon you. I won't take your virginity and leave you with the idea that there could be another. I will be your first and your last. You will have no other lovers than me. I will have no other lovers than you. You will not be my first, but you will be my last, my most precious, my most cherished. My forever love."

He's killing me. He's breaking my heart, but he's right. I'm not fully there yet. I'm afraid of getting him killed. I'm afraid of him leaving me for someone better suited for his VP stature. I'm afraid I'll come to fully rely on him and when I need him most—he'll be gone. I don't know how to trust like that. To give with abandon. To trust without limits.

His soft caress brings me back. "You're thinking too much. Let's give you something else to concentrate on." He straddles my stomach, then pulls his boxer briefs down, setting his amazing cock free. He places my hand on his shaft, moving it up and down as he slowly moves his hips. "Christ, I'm so fucking hard for you, Sweetness. I won't last long. Make me come, and then I'll get back to exploring your incredible body with my mouth."

I grip him harder.

"Yes, baby, just like that."

He's so beautiful in his raw need for my touch. It's heady to see the desire in his eyes and know I put it there.

I cup his ass. "Raise up, closer to me."

He moves closer and before he can settle back down, I lick the head of his cock, capturing a drop of cum on my tongue and swallow.

"Christ. Fuck, that's hot."

If he thinks that's hot, he's gonna love this.

I rise up and capture the head between my lips and suck as my hand pumps his shaft. I can't get all of him in this awkward position. But I manage as best I can, as best I know how, considering I've never done this before.

"Fuck, Samantha. You don't have to…ah…yes," he exclaims as I suck him deeper. He leans back, his hand finding my clit. "God, you're even wetter than before. I want you to come with me, but I'm not sure I can wait for you."

That only encourages me to make him lose his ever-loving mind, to make him as lost and overwhelmed as he made me a few minutes ago, sucking my nipples until I thought my head was going to explode.

He slowly pumps his hips as I suck and stroke him. His hands explore me, tweaking my nipples and playing with my clitoris. I'm not sure what's hotter, watching him come undone, or the words coming out of his mouth. When he starts to talk about wishing he could finger fuck me while he fucks my mouth, I lose *my* mind and come.

"Christ, look at you, sucking me even harder as you come."

I buck under him, overwhelmed by my release, but still trying to focus on him.

"Fuck, yes. I'm coming," he warns, watching me to see if I release him, but I don't. I just suck him harder, determined to taste him, to swallow everything he has to give me.

He cups my face. "Sweetness." He calls out over and over again as he shoots cum down the back of my throat.

"Holy shit, baby." He breathlessly pulls his still-hard cock from my mouth. "That..." He collapses beside me. "...was incredible."

He wraps me in his arms, and I rest my head on his chest. "Tell me again," I say softly.

He kisses my forehead and runs his hand up my back. "I love you. And not because you just sucked my cock."

I let out a sigh of contentment. "I love you too, Joseph." I may be afraid to commit to our future, to believe in forever. But one thing I know for certain—I will love him till the day I die and probably beyond. Nobody has ever seen me, or treated me like he does. I doubt anyone ever will.

He squeezes me tighter. "Say it again, Sweetness."

I smile against his chest. "I love you, Joseph."

"Those are the sweetest words I have ever heard." He rolls me over. "I love you."

He nuzzles into my neck and then moves lower, sucking on my nipples, before making it back down to my body. "Now, let me taste you. I need to feel you come on my tongue."

"Oh, Jesus, Joseph."

He laughs. "You love my dirty talk. It makes you hot." He checks out my breasts. "It made your nipples even harder. Let's see if it made you wetter."

Fourteen

Joseph

I MADE HER COME TWO MORE TIMES WITH MY
mouth. It was quite spectacular. Really.

Now my cock is painfully hard, again. I had to ditch my underwear. I roll on my back, my cock bobbing against my abdomen. She eyes it, not missing a thing, even in her sex-drunk state.

"Come sit on my face, Sweetness, and take my cock in your mouth. I need you again."

"Joseph, you're insatiable. I don't need any more. I can just take care of you." She moves to take my cock in her mouth.

I'm not having it. I lift her by her hips and laugh at her yelp as I swing her around, placing her knees on either side of my chest.

Her ass sways as she peers back at me.

"When I said I needed you again, I meant I needed *you*." I lick her wet swollen pussy. She shudders and instinctively opens her thighs to me. "I meant, I needed to taste you again. I need to feel you come. I need it more than I need you to suck me off."

"God. Joseph, the things you say." She takes me in hand and licks my cock, tip to base and back.

Christ, she's gonna kill me. Abso-fucking-lutely kill me.

I take her cue and lick her from her clit to her asshole. I run my fingers in her wetness and back to her untried rosebud, over and over again. Then circle it with my finger.

132

She stops sucking me. "Joseph?"

"Baby, I'm trying to be good here, but Christ, you push me. I'm gonna finger fuck your ass while you suck me off." I feel her clench against my fingers. "You like that, don't you, beautiful?"

She's silent, her head lying on my hip, my cock lost in her soft hair. "Sweetness, it's nothing to be ashamed of. Does it turn you on to think of me taking your ass?"

"You taking any part of me turns me on, Joseph."

"I'm happy to hear it. So, it's a yes to the ass play?"

"I want to do it to you too."

"Oh…wow…uh, I've never done that." I've thought of it.

"Me either, obviously." She giggles.

I pat her ass. "Get up a sec. I'll be right back."

She rolls off me, and I jump up, heading to the guest room to see if I can find what we need. I come back a minute later, my search successful.

I'd long since turned on the table lamp in her room, tired of not being able to see her. She's lying on the bed, not a hint of shyness left in her. I think I've sexed it out of her tonight. It's hard to hide when someone's buried between your thighs. I've never been shy about my body, but with her I've never felt this comfortable, this relaxed. I've also never been this turned on either, even after I come, I'm still hard and aching for her. I'm starting to think the only thing that will quench the beast is to sink my cock deep into her sweet pussy and feel her squeeze my release from me, one slow, tight clench after the other until we're both so wrung out we can't see straight.

She props up on her elbow. "Joseph, are you sure you don't want to call it a night? We've been at it for hours. I could just take care of you. Honest, I don't mind."

I sit beside her and run my hand down her hip and back up to cup her face. "Are you tired? I guess I got a little wrapped up in discovering you. I didn't stop to think you might be worn out."

She sits up, her breasts pressing into me. "I am tired, but that's not it. I have to get up in five hours for school." She glances away, blushing.

I lift her chin. "What's with the embarrassment? If we were in Austin, I'd be the one getting up for class. It's not a mark of your maturity to have to get up for school." She nods, and I kiss her nose. "However, I do have some good news. Fin got you out of school tomorrow. You don't have get up early. But, if you're having second thoughts about the ass play, we don't have to do it. Remember what I said, all you have to do is tell me you're uncomfortable, and it stops. There's no pressure. Ever. We're both all in, or we aren't. There's no sacrificing for the other person's pleasure. It's both of us 100%, or it's not happening. Clear?"

"Clear." She smiles widely. "No school?"

"No school." My smile meets hers.

She motions to the bed. "Shall we resume then?"

I pull her into my lap, skin to skin. How easy it would be to simply move her to straddle me and sink into her wet, welcoming pussy. I look in her eyes. "I don't know what I did to deserve you, Samantha, but I'm deeply grateful. I only pray I'm the man you need—that I'll grow to be all you'll *ever* need."

She lays her head on my shoulder. "I'm the lucky one. I pray I'll be woman enough for you and for your job."

"Sweetness, you are. Just as you are right at this moment. I will never need more than you are. I only need you to believe in me and our future."

"I'm trying."

"I know you are." I raise her face to mine. "Now kiss me, Sweets. Show me what you need."

Her lips perk up into a smile. "I think you know what I need better than I do."

I agree. "Then give me those lips and let me show you."

She presses her mouth to mine, and for a moment I just let our lips linger. But when I pinch her nipple and she gasps, I take the kiss deeper, showing her what we both need. What we both want.

Samantha

"Joseph," I pant, finding coherent thought difficult at the moment. He's kept me on edge for so long, trying to get me ready. If I'm ever going to be ready, it's now.

"Stop sucking me. Don't touch me until I tell you. Otherwise I'm going to come the second my finger slips inside you." His strained command nearly sends me over the edge.

I release him and glance over my shoulder. "Okay. What do I do?"

"Lay your head on the bed next to me. Can you do that, or is it uncomfortable?"

I move into position, my ass still in the air, as I straddle his face. *God, who would have ever thought I'd be doing this today?*

"You alright, Sweetness?"

"Yes. What's next?"

"Just relax and try not to come." His tongue runs up the length of me. "Christ, I love how you taste," he growls. "Okay, this might be a little cold."

I hear the pop and assume it's the lube he found when he left my room a bit ago. I'm not sure I want to know why he has it or where he found it. It was too quick for him to have borrowed it from Fin. Plus, Joseph was naked so I doubt he went in search of Fin. I feel Joseph's warm fingers moving over my ass a second before I feel the cold lube. His finger circles my hole, it's not uncomfortable, it actually feels kinda good, but I'm nervous about what's going to happen next. "Joseph," my voice quivers.

He kisses the inside of my thigh. "It's okay, baby. Just relax. You tell me to stop, and it stops. But give it a chance." He starts to rub my clitoris in the same motion as his finger on my ass.

It doesn't take long for my arousal to come back to life. It never left, just waited in limbo for him to touch me again. I can't help the need building in me, the need for him to fill me up, the need to have him sink his cock inside me. Now, with him teasing my ass, I have the need for more there too. I push back on his finger.

"That's it. Push again."

"Joseph, I'm gonna come." I start to shake, trying to hold it off.

He stops rubbing my clit, but continues the manipulation of my ass. My orgasm drops away but my desire is still high.

"Relax, baby." He pushes harder, and then he's there. His finger breaches my opening. I let out a moan, and he stills. "Are you okay?"

"Yeah." I try to steady my breathing, relax my muscles. I tensed up the moment he entered me, feeling both pleasure and pain.

I feel more lube, and then he pushes in again, this time the progression is much smoother and all pleasure. I moan into the bed. He's gonna make me come just from this.

"So damn sexy." He runs his lips along my thigh. I hear a plop next to me where the lube landed. "Your turn, go gentle."

I grab the bottle and move slowly to hover over his cock, so I can get to his ass. I can't help but snicker. I'm moving carefully so as not to dislodge his finger in my ass. "This is awkward." I laugh again.

"I know, it's a bit clinical at the moment. But I'm still hot as hell for you."

"It's weird. You've got your finger in my ass." I giggle. "Will I be able to look you in the eye again?"

He moves his finger, in and out. I still, experiencing the sensation of what it might feel like to have his cock inside me. I clench around him.

"You're squeezing me. Does that mean it feels good?"

"Mmmm."

"That's right. It's gonna feel even better when I'm touching your clit and you're sucking my cock, imagining it's my cock buried deep inside you."

A small moan escapes my lips, and his cock bobs against his stomach. I don't think either of us it going to last much longer.

"Then add in the fact you're going to be fucking my ass at the same time. It's kinky as hell." His voice is strained as he tenderly caresses my abdomen. "Now, get moving before I come all over myself."

I get lubed up, have him spread eagle, so I can reach his ass. I start at his perineum and work my way back. His cock twitches. With gritted teeth, he reminds me not to touch it. He's hanging on the edge, much like I am. I start to massage his ass. His moans encourage me to push harder, making his cock bob as if it's begging for attention. My insides clenches as if my vagina is begging for his cock.

I clench again, and Joseph moans, "Fuck, baby, when you squeeze me—it nearly does me in. Push harder, before I come all over us."

I'm pushing. "I'm afraid. I don't want to hurt you."

"Suck my balls, Sweetness, and then push through. I'll tell you to stop if it's too much."

I do as he asks, and before I know it, I'm sucking his cock deep and finger fucking him as he sucks and licks me, finger fucking my ass. I thought I was overwhelmed before, that was nothing compared to this act of unadulterated hedonistic decadence.

My body's on fire. I'm gonna come. I think about releasing him, to warn him. But reading my mind, he squeezes my ass cheek and sucks my clitoris without pause. As the tingle starts in my legs and works its way up, I fuck him harder and suck him deeper as I come undone. I can't scream his name, but I moan around his cock right before he unleashes his desire and comes deep in my mouth. I swallow everything he gives me and only release him when I feel his cock finally soften.

He doesn't let up on me though, he continues to lick me, his finger going deeper in my ass, and his other hand moves over my vaginal opening teasing me, raising my desire again. He squeezes another orgasm out of me, and I come so hard I actually pass out, black out, or zone out.

I come to with him carrying me to the bathroom and sinking us both into a hot bath. I can't move. I'm catatonic. Every muscle in my body feels limp and over used. I'm done. I can't even help as he bathes me, and then himself. He talks softly in my ear, soothes me, comforts me, and doesn't makes me feel like the lump of useless flesh that I am.

He gets us out, dries us off, props me up at the sink, and hands me a toothbrush with toothpaste already on it. He steps away to brush his own teeth in the sink next to me, watching me all the while to be sure I don't fall over. I'm not convinced I won't.

He finishes first and runs kisses along my neck and shoulders as his hands caress up my back and sides. The moment I'm done, he sweeps me up in his arms and carries me back to bed. After I'm settled under the covers, naked and clean, he disappears out my bedroom door with only a towel on. He comes back a few minutes later with two glasses of water. Helping me sit up, he holds the cup as I drink down the entire glass of water. He takes a few drinks of his, then offers me as sip, but I refuse and lie back down. He finishes his, placing both cups on the nightstand before crawling in bed next to me.

He spoons me from behind, our legs and limbs intertwined. He kisses my neck, caresses my hip before his hand settles on my abdomen. "Good night."

"Joseph. Love. You," I manage to eke out before I close my eyes.

"I love you too, Samantha. I'm sorry I wore you out, Sweets. But that was the most amazing night of my life."

I hum in response. He merely chuckles and pulls me closer.

I start to drift, never having felt such love in my life, either emotionally or physically. He has absolutely ruined me for all other men. If he leaves me, it will more than break me, it will devastate me.

It.

Will.

Crush.

Me.

Fifteen

Joseph

I AWAKE ALONE IN HER BED. IT TAKES ME A MOMENT to realize what happened last night was not a dream, but reality. A fantastic reality at that. I search for the clock on the nightstand. It's only a few minutes past seven. I think it was around two when we finally went to sleep. Even after all the sex play, my morning wood makes its usual appearance. I listen to see if Samantha is in the bathroom, but everything is silent. I guess this erection is going to go unsatisfied.

I sit up, swinging my feet over the side of the bed, stretching. I rise to my feet after a few moments and make my way to the bathroom. After slipping on a pair of basketball shorts and grabbing a t-shirt, I open the door and immediately hear laughter. I hear *her* laughter, specifically, and I can't help the smile occupying my face or the warmth in my belly as a result. It's good to hear her laughing and happy. I endeavor to hear more of it in the coming days.

I enter the living room and see my brothers and my woman laughing and carrying on, having a good ole time in the kitchen. I smell bacon, and can only assume she's cooking breakfast—for them. Jealousy smacks me in the face until her eyes lock on mine, and the sizzle that cracks between us is purely ours. The heat I see in her eyes and the flush moving up her chest and face is for me. Only. Me.

As if in some synchronized move, Fin and Matt look at Samantha and then turn to lock eyes on me.

"Hey, did we wake you up?" Matt says as he walks toward me.

"No. I didn't hear a thing until I opened the bedroom door," I reply as I slip on my t-shirt, still staring at Samantha, who is quickly making her way to me. My arms wrap around her the minute she's by my side. I kiss her head and relish the smell and feel of her. "Good morning, Sweetness," I softly say into her hair.

"Morning. Hungry?"

"Starving, actually." For her and for food.

"Good." She pulls back. "Let me go finish, so we can all eat together." She stands on her tiptoes and kisses my mouth all too quickly before returning to the kitchen.

I'm loving this public display of affection. I've never been much for PDA, but with Samantha, I want everyone to know she's mine. Plus, I'd never survive trying to keep my hands to myself. I can't resist her, not since I've gone full in, and especially not after last night.

Matt moves closer and gives me a hug. "So, you finally bit the bullet, huh?" He nods to Samantha. "I'm happy for you. She's the best." He pats me on the back as we walk toward the breakfast bar. "And she makes a killer breakfast."

I smile at that. "Yes, she does. I'm a little jealous you two get a home-cooked meal every morning."

Fin hands me a cup of coffee. "It's the good life. I won't deny it. I'm not going to let her move back home. My stomach would revolt."

She bumps his hip as he comes to help her. "I think you'd manage, Fin. You've survived all these years without a cook. Perhaps it's a sign you need to find a woman. Someone to fill your bed *and* your stomach." She eyes me before she continues. "And your heart. That goes for you too, Matt."

"You had me at bed and stomach, but lost me with the love stuff," Matt grumbles.

Matt is the die-hard manwhore, just like Jace. Well, maybe not like Jace anymore, who's taken it to a whole new level. But Jace is gonna have to clean up his act and focus more on school and his future career aspirations, which just might bring him to MCI to work with Matt. They are two peas in a pod in more than just their womanizing ways. They're PR twin gods and would make a remarkable team, taking MCI to a new level of marketing and public relations.

If Jace would pull his head out of his ass.

"Someday, you two will find the woman who will knock you off your feet. You won't know what to do with yourself, how to function without her." She turns and gives Matt a wink. "And more so, you won't even want to survive without her."

My stomach twists with her words. She believes Matt and Fin will find someone they can't live without, yet she doubts she is *it* for me?

She stops mid-step. My face must reveal my thoughts. As realization dawns, she sets down two plates and returns for the others, her smile and lightness of step gone.

Once we're seated and conversation flows easily, I notice she's just pushing the food around her plate, not eating, and not joining in on our conversation. I softly nudge her shoulder. She gives me a placating smile, one I don't believe for a second.

A moment later, she hops up and says quickly, "Excuse me. I'm going to shower." She turns away before I can see her face. "Leave the dishes," she says before disappearing down the hall to her room.

I glance between my brothers, embarrassed and not sure of what to say.

"What happened?" Fin asks, his fork stopped halfway to his mouth.

I shrug and scratch my head. "I think it was my reaction to what she said to you two, about finding the *one* and never letting her go."

"What? You don't think that's true for us?" Matt asks.

"No, that's not what he means," Fin interjects. "Sam thinks you and I will find the one," he says to Matt. "But she doesn't believe she's the one for Joe." Fin looks at me. "Right?"

"Yeah, basically. She either believes I won't find the one, or when I do, it couldn't possibly be her." I let out a sigh. "But fuck, it is her. She's it for me. I've told her that as recently as last night." I run my hand through my hair and then get up, taking my empty plate to the sink. I grip the counter and meet Fin's gaze. "I told her I love her. She even said it back to me."

"But, she doubts it's forever?" Fin asks, already knowing the answer.

I nod. "She doubts she's *my* forever. I don't think she doubts her feelings for me. She still thinks there's someone else out there for me, and when I find her, I'll break Samantha's heart." I lean back against the island facing them.

"Motherfucker." I close my eyes and scrub my face with my hands.

"Shit," Matt says. "I thought it was mutual with you two. It seems so obvious you're made for each other."

"We are."

"They are," Fin says at the same time.

"I have to prove it to her."

"How?" Fin asks skeptically. I swear that man can read my mind. We're so much alike.

"I could ask her to marry me."

"No," Fin says almost angrily, getting up and coming around the bar to stand in front of me. "It reeks of desperation. You already gave her a promise ring, don't mess it up by pushing before she's ready."

"I need her to believe in my commitment to her."

"Then prove it to her, day in and day out. Don't tie yourself to her with a marriage license, where she might think you're just obligated to stay with her. Convince her by being committed, through your schooling, through the distance of living in different cities. Show her you're committed in the face of no commitment. Meaning you aren't married, and you could easily cheat or go find someone else, but you won't. You don't. You stay with her because you *choose* to stay with her, not because you're tied to her through marriage."

"You're right," I agree.

"Damn straight I'm right. This is the long game, brother," Fin says.

"It's a marathon, not a sprint," I reinforce.

"Exactly," Fin nods.

"A marathon," Matt repeats with awe in his voice. I have to smile, he seems dazed and confused by all of this.

Fin laughs. "I'll explain it to you on our way to work." He pats Matt on the back. "Let me grab my laptop, and I'll be ready to go."

Matt stares at me for a minute. "So, she's the one for you?"

I nod in the affirmative.

"But, you're not going to ask her to marry you?"

I shake my head no.

"You're going to be committed with no commitment?"

"Yes."

"Alright." He gets up and surprises me with a big hug. "I'm happy for you, brother. She's perfect for you." He releases me, but keeps his hands on my shoulders. "Don't let her fuck it up."

More poignant words have never been spoken.

PART 6
UNTOUCHABLE
MAY

Sixteen

Samantha

I DON'T KNOW HOW MICHAEL, OR ANYONE WHO HAS to go undercover, pulls it off. I've only had one phone call with Roderick, my father's killer, and it made my stomach churn. I immediately felt dirty, in need of a shower. I didn't have to pretend I was only agreeing to meet him under duress, or keeping it a secret, as it is both those things. Only Joseph, Fin, Michael and his team, and Victor and his team are aware of the plan. I'm not an actress by any stretch of the imagination, and though it's still weeks away, the stress of it weighs on me daily.

There's an extra layer of secrecy between Victor and his team's involvement in areas the FBI are being kept in the dark, except Michael, who's fully vetted and in the know. I think. Honestly, Victor is probably the only one who knows everything. I'm sure he's keeping some things from Michael just to lessen the blowback when the FBI hears of Joseph, Fin, and Victor's involvement.

Per the plan they've cooked up, I'm supposed to slip away at my graduation ceremony using the massive crowd as cover. I thought for sure I'd have to convince Roderick to wait till then, figuring he'd insist on meeting sooner. He didn't take much convincing at all. I didn't even have to tell him about my 24/7 protection. He already knew. No surprise there. As much as he watched me before that fateful day, it makes sense he would continue to watch me afterwards, especially since he hasn't yet obtained the information he seeks.

I don't trust him. I would be a fool to believe he intends on letting me go. A part of me hopes there is honor even among thieves, crooks, murderers. That his word is worth something, but I don't believe that to be the case. It's a risk to meet him, to agree to be alone with him, to put myself out there, vulnerable. But I don't have a choice. Not if I want the people I love to be safe. Not if I want a chance at a normal life, not looking over my shoulder for the rest of it. And not if I want justice for my father's death.

Michael and Victor are planning on nabbing him before we even make it to the parking lot. They're not planning on me actually disappearing with him.

But I am.

I've got plans of my own I'm putting into place, as a backup of the backup of the backup. Triple redundancy. A girl can never be too prepared, especially when dealing with a man with no scruples who is an expert at evading capture.

I've pulled Scott, the head chef at work, and Sebastian into my web of lies. I elected to keep Margot out of it. She'd be more than willing to help, but I can't bring myself to put her in danger. She's got enough going on with her family troubles, and she's just a little wisp of thing. She couldn't fight a flea if she had to.

I met with Scott at work a few weeks ago. He still cooks me dinner on my breaks, so it's not unusual for us to hang out during our shifts. It didn't raise suspicion, and my protection stayed out of the kitchen, watching the doors and diners instead. I slipped into the freezer just before it shut behind Scott.

"Shit, Sam. You scared me." He glanced to the closed door. "What are you doing, girly?"

"You're ex-military, right?" I said in quick succession, afraid I'd lose my nerve.

His arms folded over his massive chest as he squinted, scrutinizing my every word. "What are you up to?"

I looked around the freezer. It seemed like such an easy idea, so simple, but now that I was standing there in front of this huge guy, who probably knew more about clandestine schemes than I could ever think to dream up—I felt downright ridiculous.

His face softened, and he cocked his head. "Tell me, Sam. What's got you all twisted up that you had to sneak in here away from your protection to ask me such a question?"

"I need your help."

His arms dropped to his sides. "Anything. What do you need?"

I took a long, steadying breath. "I need you to help me survive meeting my father's killer."

He let out a punch of air. "Fuck, baby." His head fell forward, shaking slowly side to side. He cracked his knuckles, muttering to himself.

I wasn't sure if he was contemplating helping me or contemplating throwing me out on my ass.

Suddenly, he straightened, cracked his neck and met my eyes. Decision was written all over his face. "What'd you have in mind?"

I nearly broke down and sobbed in relief. *He's gonna help me.*

Each shift we used my break to scheme, get status checks. He pulled Sebastian in, with my urging. Scott was the one to contact him, though, so Sebastian and me were never seen in direct contact with each other. During the day, they scouted out what was needed, and we finalized the plans each time I worked. We've not left any electronic trail of our interactions. Everything was in person, and anything written down was only done by Scott, as he is the most unlikely suspect since we've never associated with each other outside of work. I trust him and Sebastian explicitly.

A horn blares and jolts me in my seat.

"Sweetness?" Joseph's hand grips my leg, concern written all over his face by my overreaction.

I smile and lean against his shoulder. "Sorry. I guess I'm a little on edge after shooting practice."

His arm wraps around my shoulder, tucking me in securely at his side. His warm lips brush my temple, once…twice…three times. "I'll have to find a way to help you relax, then."

I try not to squirm in my seat. His eyes are molten green gems of desire. "How?" I feign ignorance.

His scans my face. "Christ, I love the way you blush when you're turned on." His warm lips press against mine, slowly, tenderly. I sigh, and he ensnares it, presses forward, his tongue flicking and teasing mine before his mouth captures my lips, sucking and pulling one and then the other, retreating and then going back again for more. Savoring me like a sweet wine or a cherished delicacy.

"Sir." One of Victor's men interrupts our splendor.

On a groan, Joseph pulls away, his eyes scorching me. "Hold that thought, Sweetness."

I try to catch my breath as he directs his focus to Victor and the muscle-bound guy in the passenger seat. I can't remember his name. Michael's team is behind us somewhere, never far behind. The FBI haven't sanctioned my right to practice shooting a gun, but they also haven't put a stop to it. Michael is notably absent whenever we go, which is intentional.

"Yes." Joseph's deep voice rumbles in his chest.

"We're here, sir." Huge Guy's eyes dart between the two of us. "Do you still want to go in, or do you want to pick up?"

I glance at Victor in the rearview mirror, and his knowing smirk makes me blush further. He's warmed up tremendously over the months, showing me he's actually human. Not so scary, at least with me. If he barked orders at me like he does his men, I'd pee myself. Seriously.

Joseph's hot gaze eats me up. "I believe we'll take it to go." He raises his brows in question.

I nod, nuzzling into his chest. "Yes, to go sounds perfect."

We make a picnic on the floor in my room, sitting face to face, eating out of the Chinese takeout containers. He's feeding me more than I'm feeding myself.

"Open." He holds lo mein noodles above my head, dangling from his fingers.

I open like a baby bird, taking it all in. He flicks his tongue at the corner of my mouth, catching the yummy drippings before I can swipe it away, then sits back and sucks his fingers clean.

"No need for napkins when I'm around." He arches a brow playfully. "I'll lick you clean, Sweetness."

I groan as I pop a shrimp in my mouth to accompany the noodles, more from the visual of him licking me than from the taste of the food. "Sounds delicious," I manage through my bite.

He smirks, giving me a closed-mouth kiss, his lips warm and sexy as hell.

I dangle a snow pea in front of his mouth. He holds my hand in place as he closes his lips around the end and sucks it in, in one slow, steady suck. Then, he nips my fingers before pulling them into his mouth to clean.

My insides contract. *Jeez, he's serious about the no napkin thing.*

He feeds me another bite using chopsticks this time. "Samantha, I want to talk to you about something."

"Uh oh, sounds serious," I tease.

His stoic face not giving anything way, he tilts his head. "It's a serious topic...rather intimate." His eyes light up at that admission.

Oh. It must have to do with sex for him to consider it *intimate.*

"I don't want to embarrass you, so I'm just going to ask it straight out."

"Okay," I hesitantly reply, unsure I want to hear his question.

"We haven't talked about it, and we aren't together enough for me to know for sure without asking."

So much for him asking straight out. He always says that, and then he eases me into it. He rarely just blurts out whatever the question is.

"You're on the pill, right?" His expression is uncharacteristically bashful.

"Yeah." I put down my food. I can't think about food anymore.

He's not having it, though, and holds up another bite of chicken. "Eat," my caveman commands.

I comply but ask, "Why?" before I do.

"Because you're not eating enough."

"No! Why do you want to know about me being on the pill?"

He winks. He knew what I meant. "I think you're close to trusting my commitment to you, to our future. You're not there yet, but soon, and I want to be prepared. Because when you are there, when you fully believe in me, in us, I'm making you mine." He cups my cheek and leans in, running his lips down my neck.

I tremble from the contact and the idea he's conjuring in my head.

His lips press to mine, sucking my bottom lip as he pulls away. "I don't want anything between us. I want you bare."

"Joseph," I nearly moan, closing my eyes, nipples tightening, my breath shallowing, waiting for his next move.

He runs his nose along the side of my face, nuzzling into me. "I'm clean. I was tested recently, but I've never had unprotected sex." A full body shudder has me gasping at the thought of having sex with him. *Real* sex. *Penetrating* sex.

He chuckles and kisses the corner of my closed eyelid. "Open." I open my eyes as he presents a shrimp. "Bite."

I sink my teeth in, maybe a little too aggressively, and I'm slightly disappointed it's food instead of his cock.

He smirks and pops the other half in his mouth, then kisses me. "You like that, Sweetness? The idea of my cock inside you? Bare, nothing between us, feeling me hard and needy, moving in and out of your wet heat. Making you tremble with need until you come for me, squeezing me, pulling my cum from me, filling you up."

"Jesus," I mumble, panting, heart racing, and wet as sin.

He moves the food and pulls me sideways onto his lap. Our lips crash together, and our soft, slow kisses from earlier are replaced with hot, devouring ones.

In a flash, I'm naked, stretched out across the floor, and he's buried between my thighs, his mouth devouring me in a whole other way. He's giving me pleasure, but he's taking it too, enjoying it nearly as much as me. When I finally come with an arch in my back and a scream echoing in my ears, he growls and laps up my desire as if it is his sustenance.

"I love you, Joseph," I whisper into the cavernous bliss of my orgasm.

"I know, Sweetness." He kisses my thighs. "Now, show me again how much."

His mouth returns to the warm sanctuary he insists is his new home.

Seventeen

Joseph

"**C**HRIST, JOE. SIT THE FUCK DOWN. YOU'RE EVEN making me nervous," Michael's gruff voice interrupts my thoughts.

I stop in front of the window, my hands buried in my pockets and my shoulders raised to my ears, taking in the skyline from Fin's penthouse.

"I'm gonna go crazy today. I hate her having to do this. It's like a knife to my heart that I can't be by her side the whole time. It's killing me." The anger in my voice is unmistakable.

A large hand grips the back of my neck, hard. I relish the discomfort.

"We'll be watching her, Joe. Nothing will happen to her. You have to act the part of the calm, cool, proud boyfriend, not the anxious, up-tight, out-for-murder, protective caveman you are at this very moment. If you can't do that, then you need to stay the fuck home. Your behavior could put her in jeopardy if Roderick notices. And believe me, he'll be watching you as much as he'll be watching her." Victor pats my back before stepping away.

"I got it." Over my shoulder I survey Victor and Michael's teams, the ones not in route or at the coliseum already. They're all staring at me.

Turning to fully face them, I square my shoulders, hands by my side. Solid. In control. "I won't fuck it up."

I point to every one of them. "But if she gets hurt, if one hair on her beautiful head is messed up, I'm coming after every one of you. I don't give a shit how strong, smart, and well-trained you all *think* you are. She. Is. My. Life. I will take you all down if you jeopardize that."

They could have laughed in my face. The protective boyfriend lashing out, making idle threats. But there is nothing idle about my threat. I mean every word, and if it takes me to my dying breath, I will make good on it. Maybe it's my size, the power in my voice, or the determined set in my stance, but not one of them laughs, smirks, or dismisses my threat. I get curt nods or *understoods* from each of them.

After a quick word and disbursement of his team, Michael saunters over. He stands shoulder to shoulder with me as I peer out the window once again. "You would have made an excellent commander, Joe. I think you missed your calling."

I think he's being a smartass, as usual, but his earnest gaze surprises me. He's looking at me with admiration, maybe. My anger dissipates instantly. "You won't let her out of your sight." Not a question.

"Not for a heartbeat," he replies with the confidence I need to hear.

I glance at my watch. "Let me have a minute with her before we leave."

He nods. "Fifteen."

"Knock when you're ready." I don't wait for his reply. I disappear down the hall.

I rap on the door before entering to give a heads-up, not to ask for permission to enter. I'm in no mood to be turned away. I need my girl.

She's standing in front of the full-length mirror. The mirror I had her stand naked in front of only last night as I brought her to orgasm, twice. Once with my fingers and then again with my mouth.

Her eyes catch mine in the mirror. The blush creeping up her skin tells me she's thinking of last night too.

I stalk closer, bracketing her back, my lips graze and suck gently at the nape of her neck. "You look beautiful, Samantha." All dressed in black: black dress, black pumps. Simple, classy, and sexy as hell.

She sighs and leans into me. "Thank you." She hugs my arms encircling her waist, her eyes wary as she studies my reflection. "What is it, Joseph?"

Buck up, asshole. She needs you strong and confident.

I turn her around so I can see the face of the woman I love beyond words. I cup her cheek and kiss her rosy lips before answering. I don't want to rehash my concerns, my fears over her being used as bait.

"Be careful. Focus. Be smart. Be strong." I close my eyes as I wrap her in a tight embrace, pressing my lips to her forehead. "Come back to me." I say it as much as a command to her as a prayer to God and the universe at large.

She squeezes me tightly, not letting up. "Always."

Samantha

I grip my hands to stop their shaking. I've got to get a handle on my nerves. I was doing alright until Joseph had to leave to take his seat with the rest of his family. I'm thankful for the McIntyres and all they've done for me, my mom, and even Jace. They're my second family, but honestly, I feel more a part of their family than my own.

What would it be like to *truly* be in their family? It's a thought I've become more comfortable with and one I've allowed myself to dwell on more and more. It doesn't seem so a farfetched any longer, the idea of Joseph and me together for the long haul.

He's been my steady rock since my dad died. We've had our ups and downs, many self-inflicted by me and my meager attempt to squash our relationship before it took flight. I'm beginning to believe we were always destined to be from our very first breathtaking hello. I've been a fool for trying to stop it, such wasted time and heartache.

"Sam."

That familiar voice makes me jump. I turn, surprised to see Jace standing at the doorway.

My mom's not here. She's still at the center she's been in for months now, trying to find herself in the midst of her sorrow over living without my dad. I didn't know if Jace was coming today. He's been his normal-since-dad-died distant self.

"I didn't think you were coming." I don't try to hide my anger. It's been hard not having him around, and I resent the fact he's even here now, pretending he wants to be.

He frowns and steps in the room, glancing at Michael and then back at me. "It's your graduation. Why wouldn't I be here?"

"For the same reason you haven't been around for the last three months. You don't care."

He steps closer, hurt etched along his face. "I do care. Jesus, I've really fucked things up with us, haven't I?"

You think? Asswipe. "What do you think?"

He runs his hand nervously through his dark hair. "I think you're mad at me and have every right to be."

"Well, now that we're in agreement, you can leave. I've got a speech to get ready for, and I don't need you in here undermining my confidence and making me more nervous," I spew in one heated breath, sick to my stomach for having said it so harshly.

His wide-eyed shock tells me my words hit home, exactly how I intended them to. "I'm sorry, Sam. I truly am. At the risk of making it worse, I've got something I need to tell you."

I pace away from him, glancing at Michael, hoping he'll throw Jace out.

Michael's raised brows confirm he'll in fact do just that if I want him to.

I stop. *Do I want him to?*

"Michael, can you give us a minute?" Jace asks.

I don't glance back at Jace, but it's obvious there's unsaid tension between the two of them by the contempt on Michael's face.

"Actually, Jace, I can't," Michael bites out a little too happily as he crosses his arms over his chest, standing in front of the closed door. He's playing the protector to the hilt with no plans to give an inch.

Maybe not to Jace, but he might for me. "Can you wait in the hall?" I ask softly.

Michael sighs. "Fine. But you only have about twenty minutes before this dog and pony show commences."

I thank him as he slips out the door, giving a menacing scowl to Jace.

"What's that about? You piss off Michael too?"

He shrugs. "Apparently, but really, how can you tell? He's always got his panties in a twist over something."

I can't help but smile—it's true. Michael is intense and brooding, and seems pissed off about something most of the time. Though, I have seen a softer side of him, one I don't imagine many get to see. Things have been different between us since he shared his heartache over losing his Gracie, but I'm not about to betray the trust he's afforded me by mentioning to Jace that he's not always hard as nails.

I sit down on the lone couch in the room. There are two other chairs, but they don't look all that comfortable. I wonder if any famous people have stayed in this room while waiting to go out on stage. I guess this is a dressing room. There are a few others in this hall, but this is the one Michael sequestered to keep me separate and safe from all the hustle and bustle going on behind the scenes as they ready for our graduation ceremony. I'm just a small player in the ceremony, and imagine I wouldn't have such accommodations if I wasn't in the situation we're in now.

"Congratulations on Valedictorian, by the way." Jace's voice brings me back to him.

"Thank you."

"Are you nervous?"

"Very. You know I don't like being the center of attention. I'd rather be home right now than walk across that stage to get the diploma I've worked so hard for, much less getting ready to make a speech." Maybe I'll just skip it altogether and move up the timetable in meeting Roderick. It'd be a good excuse to not have to give my speech or stand up in front of all those people.

"You'll do good. I have every confidence in you, Sam."

I nod but don't respond. If he wants to talk after all this time, he's going to have to make the effort.

He sits in the chair closest to me. His leg bounces with nerves. "I've been a shitty brother since dad died. I plan to make it up to you. We can talk about it whenever you want to. But right now, I need to tell you how I was a shitty friend to Joe and in turn an even shittier brother to you."

That sounds even more ominous than those four dreaded words, *we need to talk.*

His hands squeeze the armrest until his fingertips are white. Not a good sign.

I glance at the clock. He's running out of time. "You'd better move it along."

He follows my motion to the clock and nods in understanding. Taking a deep breath, he proceeds to remind me of one of the worst nights of my life, the night I broke up with Joseph.

"He ended up at the bar in the middle of my shift. I didn't have a clue why you would break up with him. And to be honest, I didn't really care. I was too deep in my own shitstorm to see beyond myself. All I could think about was who I was gonna fuck after work." He looks chagrined and unsettled as he continues. "Tiff was there, one of the chicks I've been with in the past. More than once. I knew if Joe said the word, she'd be all over him, more than willing to help him forget his troubles."

My chest tightens, and my stomach lurches. "Stop." I hold up my hand. I can't hear this. I can't hear how Joseph and *Tiff* got together. I could have died happily never knowing her name.

He moves to sit on the coffee table in front of me. "No, I can't stop. You need to hear this."

159

No, I really don't.

"He wasn't interested, Sam. He chastised me for even mentioning another woman to him, for thinking he would even be interested in fucking another woman."

I close my eyes. "Please, stop saying that word."

"What? Fucking?" He seems confused.

"Yes! You talk about it like it's no big deal, like it doesn't mean anything. Yet for some of us, it means…everything." Shakily, I wipe the tears from my cheek.

He leans forward, his arms braced on his thighs, his face buried in his hands. "I wish I knew what that felt like. For me, it doesn't mean anything. Not anymore…if it even ever did."

"Jesus, Jace. What happened to you?"

His hands fall away, the weariness in his face and eyes so apparent. He's lost.

"I wish I knew." He sits up and squares his shoulders. "We're getting sidetracked. I'll try to curb my language." His small, sweet smile reminds me of the boy I used to know, which makes my heart ache for him all the more.

"The bottom line is, he blew off my suggestion. All he wanted from me the rest of the night were shots to drown out his misery. Once I got off work, I got him home and into bed. He could hardly walk or speak clearly, he was so drunk. I knew he was gone, out for the count."

Shit. Here comes a *but.*

"I asked Tiff to follow us home driving his car, and I'd get her a cab home. Ended up, one of her friends drove her car to our house. One thing led to another and me and her friend disappeared to my room, but before I closed the door I directed Tiff to Joe's door telling her to make him forget."

"Oh my god, Jace! He told you he wasn't interested, and yet you sent her into his room knowing good and well he was too drunk to probably even say no." I push away from him, needing distance and motion to calm my raging anger and racing heart.

Joseph didn't choose her. He didn't purposely seek out another woman to have sex with.

"I told you I was a shitty friend. The thing is, the next morning, he had no recollection of what happened. He didn't remember Tiff at all. He thought it was a dream. A dream of you, Sam. Not Tiff. When he saw evidence of what happened…that it was real…that it wasn't you, he was devastated and angry as fuck at me."

I stop my pacing. "Evidence?"

He stands and faces me. "Tiff likes to scratch. Leave her mark."

Jesus.

Joseph let me think it was his choice, but he didn't choose her. He thought it was me and that it was just a dream. Why? He lied to protect Jace? All this time he's been carrying this around, apologizing to *me* for something he didn't do. Apologizing for something that was done to *him.*

Speechless. I'm speechless and angry as fuck.

"Get out."

Joseph

I'm beyond tired of waiting for this day to be over. I see Jace making his way to our seats a moment before the ceremony begins. I'm not happy to see him, but I am happy he pulled his head out of his ass long enough to be here for her. It's bad enough her mom couldn't make it. Him being here is some consolation, I suppose.

My phone vibrates in my hand. I didn't bother to put it in my pocket. I don't want to chance missing a call or text from Samantha, Victor, or Michael.

I'm elated to see it's a text from my girl.

Samantha: *I'm all in, Joseph. I choose you. All of you. Always. I'm yours today, tomorrow. Forever.*

My heartrate increases as pure joy spreads to fill every empty crevice, secret dream, and distant visions of our future. *Our* future. Together. That revelation, momentarily soothing the anxious beast in me.

Me: *You have no idea how happy I am to hear that. I'm all yours too. Today. Tomorrow. Forever. My love. My Sweetness.*

She doesn't text back, and I don't expect her to as everyone is filing onto the stage. I'll see her any moment taking her position with the other officiates. As much as I hate not being by her side, I at least get to see her beautiful face sitting on that stage and know she's safe while she's up there. Mere moments pass and those on the stage finally settle.

I scan the stage, starting to get that tingle on the back of my neck. Something's not right. I don't see her. Everyone's seated, and there's an empty chair on the stage. A few of the staff look around, conversing, trying to figure out where she is, I imagine.

Dread fills me.

Something's wrong.

I glance to the nearest FBI agents and see a few are already on the move. I make eye contact with Victor's man, my man, and he motions to me one second before I get another text.

Michael: *She's gone.*

PART 7
HIDING IN PLAIN SIGHT

Eighteen

Joseph

I STORM TOWARD MICHAEL. "WHAT THE FUCK DO you mean she's gone?"

Michael squares his shoulders, braces for the shit storm I'm about to unleash. "She was talking to Jace. Then I escorted her to the stage with the others. She passed behind a curtain, following in the order they would sit on stage. Two seconds later, she's gone." He runs his hand nervously through his hair, actually pulling hard at the end of the motion. I know that move. It gives a little twinge of pain and lets you know if you're not dreaming.

Fuck. I wish this were only a bad dream.

"Calm, Joe. She needs you calm and collected." Fin's soothing voice comes from behind. I turn and see Fin on his phone. He raises his pointing finger to me telling me to wait just a second.

Fuck!

I scan the area. It's total chaos with FBI agents scrambling around backstage checking every door, nook and cranny. I move to start to search myself, but I stop when I realize it's only Michael's men searching. Where are Victor's men, my men?

A second glance at Fin has him motioning me to follow him.

We make a few turns backstage. I stop cold when I see he's leading me out a door marked EXIT. I'm not leaving if there's a possibility she's still in this building.

165

Fin drops his phone in his pocket. "We need to go. She's not here." He says it with such certainty, my solidly planted feet move quickly to close the distance between us.

"How do you…the trackers?"

"Yep." He looks back over his shoulder before pushing me through the door.

The bright light of the mid-morning sun blinds me momentarily.

"There," he shouts as he starts to run down the long alleyway heading toward a ramp.

Without a second thought, I follow, reaching the top a few seconds behind Fin and stop in my tracks when I see a black SUV with Victor at the helm. Fin dives in the back, leaving the door open for me. I climb in. I need to know what the hell's going on and why the men I'm paying aren't in the coliseum searching for Samantha along with the FBI.

Victor speeds off before I even get my door closed.

"She's with Sebastian," Victor advises, then turns his attention to his man in the passenger seat who's looking at his laptop.

A few quiet interactions later, Victor's attention is back on me. "Your sweet innocent Sam has been hatching her own plan. She has no intention of falling prey to Roderick. She's been in cahoots with Scott, that chef from her job, and Sebastian."

"What? For how long? And how the fuck do you know this?" I bark, my patience long gone.

Victor glances at me in the review mirror. "When you asked me to protect her, I investigated her co-workers and found out Scott is ex-military. I approached him, got him on the payroll. His job was to keep an eye on her at work. It wasn't much of a stretch for him. He'd already been doing that—he and the other big guy there, Bruce. They watched out for her after Roderick started showing up and displaying stalker-type tendencies. They walked her to her car each night, basically already playing the job of protection. I just made it official. And it let Sam think she had one place with a little extra slack—the illusion of freedom from her security team. Nothing interesting came of it until Roderick reached out to her."

"The letter?" I ask.

"Yep. That and the plan to use her as bait sent her self-preservation skills into overdrive. She got Scott and Sebastian on board early, but the plan didn't fully come to fruition until Michael put today's plan in motion. She knew we'd have protection everywhere. I suspect she feared Roderick would bring in extra men and it could turn into a blood bath. She set up her own plan to meet with Roderick on her terms, on her timetable."

I lean forward, close enough to bite his ear off. "Why the fuck am I just now hearing about this?"

Samantha

I slip into the back of the car, my head down. "Any trouble?"

"Nope. All's smooth in the world of Operation Babycakes." Sebastian chuckles at his pet name for our plan.

"You know, it doesn't sound very foolproof, or well-planned, calling it 'Operation Babycakes.' Why not something more menacing?"

"Because it needs to seem innocent and not all clandestine cloak and danger type shit." He takes a sharp right out of the parking lot heading onto the main road.

I let out a deep breath of relief. Phase One, complete.

Pulling out my phone, I quickly text Roderick.

Me: *Change of plans. Meet me at Micky's Burger Joint. 20 mins.*

Instead of replying in text, he calls me, as I anticipated he would. "Hello."

"What the hell are you trying to pull, Sam?" His accent is thicker and still unrecognizable to me.

"I'm not trying to pull anything." I let out a sigh and hope he buys

167

my exasperation. "I got spooked, okay? It's not like I do this every day. There were too many of them. You never would have been able to get to me. I saw an opening, and I took it. I ditched my detail. I'm on my way to Micky's now. Are you coming or not?"

After a long beat and two heavily exaggerated sighs, he finally agrees. "I'll be there."

I hang up without a goodbye. I look up at Sebastian and shrug. That's what they do in the movies. There's no pleasant goodbyes when talking to bad guys.

"Why aren't you using your burner phone?" Bash asks.

"Because I don't want Roderick to think I'm smart enough to get a burner phone. Plus, I want my guys to track me and listen to the calls. I'm not hiding anything from Michael and Victor. I just needed to be in control of how this goes down, be a few steps ahead of them. Roderick thinks I can get him what he needs, and as long as he keeps believing that, I have the advantage. But I need Michael and Victor to be there when my advantage runs out." Which it will. It's just a matter of time.

"But you don't have a clue where the information is, do you?" Bash asks over his shoulder.

"I actually do. I have a feeling. I'm not sure, but I suspect." I stare out the window and my mind races to Joseph. "It doesn't matter, though. I just need to give Michael a chance to catch up to us. My goal is not to give Roderick what he wants. My goal is to get justice for my father's death." And keep Joseph and everyone else safe.

My phone still in my hand, I send Joseph a text.

Me: *Find me, but stay out of sight. I will run if I see you. I can't lose you. One of us in danger is enough. Trust me. I love you.*

Joseph: *If the roles were reversed, would you let me do this on my own?*

Me: *Yes, if you felt it was the only way. I wouldn't want to distract you worrying about me while doing something so dangerous. Besides, I'm not alone, am I?*

Joseph: *No, Sweetness, you're not. Never alone. I'll do it your way for now, but I'll come for you when the time is right.*

Me: *I'm counting on it. Tell me you love me. Tell me I'm yours.*

Joseph: *Sweetness. I love you more than life. I'm Yours. You're Mine. Don't get hurt.*

Me: *Same goes. Keep this number 555-563-6726*

"Pull over, Bash. This is where you get out." I collect my purse and backpack from the backseat and set them in the passenger seat.

"I don't like the idea of leaving you alone, Sam. It's not my car I'm worried about. It's you."

I grip his shoulder. "I know and I appreciate it, I do. But I have to do this without distraction. If you're with me, I won't be able to solely focus on what needs to get done. I'll be worrying about you. You're helping me in the way I need you to."

He pulls over.

I hop out. "Call Scott. He'll come get you."

"Wait. He doesn't know I picked you up?" He's surprised, but I had to keep them in the dark on some things.

"No. He's working for Victor. I had to be sure I could get out of there without an entourage." I squeeze his arm and give him a quick kiss on the cheek. "Hopefully, this will all be over soon."

Not one for quick goodbyes, he pulls me into a hug. "Be careful, babycakes. Don't get dead."

"I'll do my best." I hand him an envelope with Joseph's name on it.

He furrows his brow, confused.

"Just in case." I quickly move around to the driver's door.

"Sam." His worry is nearly more than I can bear.

"Don't, Bash. Please." I can't afford to get emotional now. I gesture to his hand. "Just hold on to it. You can give it back to me when I see you again."

"Go get 'em, Sam," he says with renewed determination.

With a nod and a parting wink, I hop in his car and drive off.

Nineteen

Joseph

I'M STILL PISSED AT VICTOR'S RESPONSE WHEN I asked why I didn't know about all of this.

Instead of being threatened by me, Victor just chuckles. "Because you're too emotionally invested. I couldn't take the chance of you pushing her to tell you her plan or trying to stop it. She needs that confidence, believing she has a leg up over Roderick. He'll never suspect what she's done. It's not much. It's basically a bunch of redundancies. Scott and Sebastian did the leg work, since she couldn't get out from the eye of her protection, so she had to rely on them. They set up different touch points between the coliseum and her father's office and then seemingly random locations around town just in case she needed a place to go. In each location, they drafted two employees to keep an eye out for her today. The watcher's job was simply to send a text message to a burner phone with the time and location she was spotted and if someone else was with her. She also had them stash weapons, so she could arm herself after Roderick ensured she wasn't armed. But to be honest, I wasn't aware of her plan to escape today on her own. Scott was in the dark too, or he's playing double agent. For his sake, I hope that's not the case."

I can't believe she pulled this off on her own, or nearly on her own. I slip my phone in my pocket, knowing I won't be hearing from her anytime soon. She's made her move. Now she just needs us to follow her, keeping an eye on her movements, keeping her safe from a distance. I'm not crazy about it, but we don't have much of a choice if we want to catch this guy.

Victor pulls into a parking space across the street and down from Mickey's, the location Samantha's numerous trackers are showing her to be. We sit in silence, all four of us watching the laptop screen for any sign of movement.

"Do we have eyes in there?" I ask.

"Yes, two agents. Michael and his team are on their way," Victor responds. "And he's pissed off, thinking we knew about her plan to disappear today. I tried to tell him it was as much a surprise to me too, but he's not buying it." He shrugs a shoulder, blowing off Michael's accusations.

"Do you think Roderick has any additional people working with him?" Fin asks.

"I doubt it. He's managed to evade capture primarily because he's kept such a low profile since the shooting. I'm sure he could use the help, but it makes it harder for him to fly under the radar if he starts hiring goons. He's burned most of his bridges over the years, and the FBI aren't the only ones looking for him. Anyone he brings in now is a huge unknown for him. Not worth the risk, if he's smart. He's a lone wolf kinda guy. I think this is a one-man operation." Victor holds up his hand, stopping any further conversation as he answers his phone.

I continue to watch the laptop screen. Immediately one dot disappears, and before I can question it, another one disappears, and then another one. I start to panic, but Victor's man whispers over his shoulder. "We expected this. It's a good sign. He searched her and found the trackers we thought he would, but he didn't find all of them." He points to the remaining blips. "We're good. We only need one."

My phone vibrates. As I dig it out of my pocket, I see it's a call from Michael. I answer, but don't get a word in before he lets loose on me.

"Did you fucking know?"

I can't help but smirk. Shit's gonna fly before this day is over. "No, man. I had no idea. You think I would've been freaking out if I had? I wouldn't have even wasted any time with you. I would have been following her. You know I'd be with her if I had my way, and not let her put herself in further danger with her secret plan."

I can feel the waves of fury rolling off him. "I can't believe she fucking did this. Have you heard from her?"

"She sent me a text a about ten minutes ago." I fill him in on the gist of our text exchange as it applies to the case, not about the stuff related to our personal relationship. I also give him the new number she gave me, though I don't think it's trackable, assuming it's a burner phone.

"I guess her planning on us coming for her when the time is right is something. Now we just have to wait and see when that is and where they'll be heading next." He's calmer. Thinking instead of reacting.

"If I had to guess, I think they'll go to her dad's office," I suggest. "But why wait? Why not just go in there and get him? It's a public place, but I have no doubt one of your guys could get close enough to put a gun to his head before he even knows you're there."

"I've considered it. What if he has a gun pointed at Sam under the table? You don't think he anticipates we're following them? He may not know we're here now, but he knows we'll find her eventually, and when we do, you better believe he will use Sam however he sees fit to ensure his own survival."

"Then why the fuck did you put her in this dangerous situation?" My heart is pounding so badly, my head is starting to hurt.

"Because we need to catch him. Because she was in danger long before her father was shot. Because he never would've let this go. He's hellbent on revenge, and he sees Sam as the key. She either helps him, or he'll eliminate her and move on to Jace or Eleanor. Whoever is closest and likely to be the most useful."

"Fuck."

"I know, man. I made you a promise, and I'm gonna keep it. She's not going to be harmed. I'll do everything in my power to keep her safe." He means within his job description or not. He's already proved he's more loyal to us than to the U.S. Government. "Stay with Victor. I'll be in contact with him from here on out. When I see you next, this will be over."

God, I sure hope so.

⌒♡⌒

Samantha

You can do this. Be strong. This is about getting revenge for Dad and keeping everyone safe. This guy can't read your mind. Act cool. You can do this.

I take a cleansing breath and continue the running dialog in my head, if for no other reason than to not think about how scared I am or how badly things could go wrong.

I park in the back, taking a minute to delete all my text messages from my phone, closing out apps, and then slip it into an outside pocket in my backpack. I'm sure he won't let me keep it, hence deleting all recent activity, but I want him to think I don't have a clue. If I leave it in my car, it shows I knew he wouldn't let me keep it. If I have it on me, and he's the one to take it from me, then I come across as a dumb girl who doesn't know any better. I need him to believe the latter.

I slip my driver's license and some cash into my backpack, then slip the rest of my cash in my bra along the side band, hoping he won't search me in great detail. I'm fairly certain he'll take my cash from the backpack. I grab some lip balm, gum, and a bottled water and tuck them into the backpack. I then put my purse on the floor board in back, throwing a jacket over it. I hope it won't raise suspicion if I don't bring it with me. I think he'll buy I just didn't want to carry both.

I'm sure Michael and Victor have trackers in my purse, but I'm sure they have others in my backpack, or my clothing, or shoes. If not, I'm screwed for them being able to follow me. They wouldn't tell me where the trackers are in case my reaction while being searched gave anything away and made Roderick suspicious.

As much as I'm relying on my guys to be able to track me, I'm also prepared to go this alone. That's why I've taken all the precautions I have. If all else fails, I have to be able to save myself.

The door closes behind me, and I blink a few times before my eyes adjust to the darkened interior of Mickey's. I scan the dining room, spotting him where else but at the bar, his gaze boring holes into me. I take a deep breath and head over.

You can do this, I chant, ignoring my racing heart.

"Sam." He nods and pulls out the barstool to his right. "Nice of you to join me." He's all cocky grin and confidence. He thinks he's got this in the bag.

"I wish I could say the same." I don't have to pretend to like this guy. He would be more suspicious if I did. I sit next to him and start to place my bag in the seat next to me.

"I'll take that." He nabs my backpack and starts to rifle through it. He pulls out my phone, setting it on the bar and then pockets my cash. "We'll need this shortly." He ignores my lip balm, hair tie, and loose change in the outer pockets. "What's in here?" he asks as he starts to go through the main compartment.

"A change of clothes. I'm not running around with you in this dress and pumps."

His eyes rove my body, then he hands me my pack. "Change."

It only takes a moment before I realize he's following me to the women's restroom. Right before I get to the door, I whip around and face him. "You are not coming in here with me."

His momentary surprise disappears in a smirk. "No, I'm not. But, there is something I need to take care of first." He steps into my space, pulling the backpack from my shoulder, dropping it on the floor.

"Arms out," he demands. He runs his hands along my upper body.

I close my eyes and turn my head to the side. "I'm not going to hurt you, Sam. I just need to be sure you're not wired or carrying a weapon." His hands cup my breasts, pausing a little too long to be merely searching me.

I open my eyes and face him.

He's openly smiling at me. "Nice."

Jesus. I'm gonna be sick.

I leer at him. "If you're done feeling me up, can I go change now?"

He scans down my body. "Not just yet." His hands move down, across my abdomen and my legs.

"Turn," he orders.

I sigh and quickly turn around, facing the wall—the quicker I obey, the quicker this will be over.

His hands begin moving back up my legs, which is completely unnecessary since I'm wearing a dress, and he can plainly see I don't have any weapons or wires strapped to my legs. But it doesn't stop him from moving in closer as he runs his hands between my thighs and then up over my ass.

"Nearly done." His hot breath over my neck causes my stomach to convulse.

I manage to stay still and not show any reaction.

His hands move over my back, up to my shoulders, and I wince when he squeezes my right shoulder just a little too hard.

"Still sore?" I'm surprised to hear remorse in his voice.

"What do you care?"

He harrumphs. "I know you don't believe me, but I truly never meant to shoot you or your father."

I push back and turn around, facing him. "Enough!" I step into the bathroom, holding the door open. "Here." I lift up my dress to above my waist, revealing my bare legs and panties, then turn around, pausing, closing my eyes and swallowing, giving him time to see I'm not wired or armed.

Dropping my dress, I turn to face him. "Satisfied?"

He backs up, his hands in the air. "Yes." He nods and actually manages to look chagrined.

I grab my backpack off the floor and let the bathroom door close behind me. I lock myself in the large stall on the end and quickly get to the business of changing clothes and securing my safety. I take the opportunity to use the bathroom while I lift up the large trashcan in the stall with me. A small bag falls free from the bottom. Pride wells up seeing my planning pay off.

I quickly take out my change of clothes, slip off my shoes and dress, and put them in my backpack. I slide on my jeans, socks, tennis shoes. But before I put on my shirt, I open the hidden bag and take out what I really need: the burner phone, a small pocket gun that fits in my bra, another that straps to my ankle, and extra cash. I'm most nervous about the ankle strap, hoping he doesn't try to search me again.

I turn on the burner phone and quickly text Joseph. "I love you." And another text to Scott and Sebastian's burner phones. "Phase 2 complete." I then put the phone on mute, not vibrate as I don't want it making any sound. I slip it in my bra. It's a tiny phone and sits in the opposite cup of my bra than where I placed the gun, evening out the additional bulk on both sides. Thankfully, the padded cups easily hide the unusual shaping. Plus, I'm wearing a loose-fitting black shirt doing little to show off my figure.

After stowing the now-empty hidden bag back under the trashcan, and the extra cash and my ID in my jeans, I check my watch and see only seven minutes have passed. I quickly wash my hands.

When I step into the hall, I'm surprised Roderick isn't there waiting. I start toward the bar, but I'm grabbed by the arm with a quick jerk in the other direction. "This way, Sam."

Outside the back door, he demands, "Ditch the backpack."

"What. Why?"

He pauses a moment before answering. "Less baggage." He takes it from me and readies to dump it into a large trash bin.

"Wait!"

He scowls, and I plead my case. "I need a couple of things. My keys, lip balm, and sunglasses."

"You don't need your sunglasses and lip balm."

"Okay, but if you want to get into my dad's office without setting off the alarm I need my keys."

He shoves the backpack at me. "Fine. Be quick about it."

Joseph

"They're on the move," Victor advises his team via the ear bud and mic hanging from his ear. His eyes are on the laptop as we see two trackers head off, leaving three behind.

"She only has two left," I whisper.

Fin's hand grips my arm as Victor replies, "I doubt she'll lose those two."

While I appreciate his confidence, I'm not feeling as sure as he is. "Why are we just sitting here? Shouldn't we be on our way, for fuck's sake?"

"We don't want to spook him. My guys are on them. The three of us are too recognizable to stick close." I assume he's referring to himself, Fin, and me, since I don't even know this other guy's name. "We have to let mine and Michael's team handle the close game."

My head hits the back of the seat. This waiting is killing me. I want to get out and run after her and beat the shit out of Roderick for what he's done to her. It's already been over an hour since she escaped by herself. Every minute I'm away from her, my need to be near her grows.

Fuck me. A horrible thought comes to mind. "Is he...what's his MO? Does he have a history with sexual assault or anything like that?"

Victor's eyes meet mine in the rearview mirror. "No. No history," he says firmly. "He's actually known for being good to his wife before she died. He was raised by his mother and two older sisters. He has a daughter nearly Sam's age. I don't think he'd hurt her in that way, Joe."

Well, that's a relief. Roderick might not hurt her in *that* way, but that doesn't mean he won't hurt her, as he's already proven by shooting her.

I close my eyes and focus on my girl, willing her to be safe, strong, and brave, and most of all, to come back to me.

Fuck this.

"I'm going to go crazy if I just sit here." I lean up, talking to Victor. "Let me go to the bank where her father has a safety deposit box. If they don't find anything at her dad's office, the bank will be the next stop. Let me go there with one of your guys. We'll give the manager a heads-up about what might be coming their way. Let me be there for her if they show up." I'm not really asking for permission. I need to be in motion. Give my brain something to focus on, something proactive to do.

He glares between Fin and me. "Okay, but no heroics. My guy will have the name of who you need to speak to. We had a feeling Roderick might end up there, so this won't be news to them."

After one of Victor's men drives up, we have a brief rundown on how this is going to play out. The decision is made—Fin will accompany me, which I'm sure is only to keep me calm and stop me from doing something stupid.

I hop out of the car with a quick, "I'll call you with updates," from Victor.

"I'm counting on it. Every step, Victor," I confirm as Fin and I get in the back of another car, and make our way to the bank to ease the path Samantha may need to take to get back to me.

PART 8
RECKONING

Twenty

Samantha

LIFE CAN BE SURREAL SOMETIMES. THE WAY I SAW this day going was more cloak and dagger and not so much shopping for clothes with the man who killed my father. He's not hurried, nervous, or even seemingly concerned about being followed. It's like this is an everyday occurrence for him.

I'm still in a daze by the time we exit the store with every piece of my clothing down to my socks and shoes completely new, even my bra and panties. If shopping for underwear with my father's killer isn't icing on the weird-cake, then I don't know what is.

Thankfully, he didn't insist on going in the changing room with me, therefore, I was able to re-secure all of my hidden paraphernalia. Doubly thankful, he hasn't searched me again. Maybe he feels safe now that my clothing's been replaced with items that couldn't have been tampered with.

He insists I drive his car since I'm more familiar with the roads to my dad's office. Somehow, I doubt that. His stalking skills would ensure he knows the route backwards and forwards. I don't argue, though. Holding onto the wheel gives me a sense of power, like I control where we're going, even though I don't, and the gun in his waistband ensures I remember that.

"Why are you after this man?" I blurt.

His sad eyes meet mine for a moment before I focus back on the road. "He killed my son."

Woah. "I'm sorry. How old was he?"

"He was twelve, nearly thirteen. Now it's just Rebecca and me." His sorrow is palpable, making me feel sorry for him.

"Is Rebecca your wife?"

"No, my daughter. My wife is no longer with us."

I silently question what *'no longer with us'* means, like divorced and moved away, or no longer alive.

He seems to understand. "My wife is dead."

Jesus, this just keeps getting sadder.

"I'm really sorry for the loss of both your wife and your son." I mean it in all sincerity. I can sympathize.

"Thank you. I know you have some idea of what it is like to lose a loved one." He catches my eye when I stop at the next light. "I honestly had no intention of killing you or your father. I am deeply sorry for what happened. You must understand this man took my son and my wife from me. I will not stop until I have justice." His demeanor quickly changed from sorrow and remorse to angry and vengeful.

This angry, vengeful man is the one I need to remember is there, just below the surface. Some part of him may truly be sorry for killing my father and shooting me, but the greater part of him is what I see before me. He's the one who won't hesitate to squash me or anyone I love standing in his way. I see the depth of his despair is what drives his revenge, its fuel a never-ending furnace feeding the flames of vengeance.

I.

Cannot.

Forget.

That.

Samantha

This is the hard part, convincing Roderick I have some idea what I'm doing. Looking for something I'm quite sure is not here. I don't know how much he knows about me, so I can't play the dumb card too much, but it doesn't stop me from trying to sidetrack him with a wild-goose chase.

There's no way to distinguish the government surgeries from his normal ones. It's not like they're stamped TOP SECRET. We spend an hour separating out the male patient files within the last year—that's when Roderick believes the surgery took place on the man he's looking for. I make a stack for him to review while I move onto the reception area to go through the computer files.

My father's laptop isn't here, and I can only assume the authorities have it as evidence. However, under the office manager's desk is a hidden server I installed for my dad years ago to make backups of his files whether he was in the office or at home.

I turn on both the receptionist's computer and the server.

As I'm waiting for the computers to boot up, I realize Roderick's sequestered in my dad's office, and I'm out front, out of his eyesight. There is nothing to keep me from running out the front door and the FBI coming inside to get him. It would probably be a battle to the death, as he'd be a caged animal. Maybe that's what he deserves, but I don't want him to get suspicious.

"The computer is taking forever to boot up." I don't tell him about the backup server in case I actually find something. I have no intention of actually handing over the patient's file and putting another person's life on the line. I stick my head in my dad's office.

Roderick is sitting on the floor going through file after file.

"How did your wife die?" He didn't say the man he's after killed his wife, but he mentioned blaming the man for both deaths.

In his frustration, he doesn't even look up. He hasn't even

acknowledged me, and for a moment, I think he's going to ignore me, which may not be a bad thing. I start to head down the hall to check on the computer when his voice draws me back.

"She was never the same after our son's death."

Rightfully so. Losing a child is traumatic. Losing a child in a tragic way, even more so.

I stand quietly in the doorway, not moving, not distracting him from his thoughts.

"We tried to have another child, but she was too old to conceive. We tried fertility treatments, which didn't work, and the extra hormones made her sorrow even greater." His eyes close as he continues to speak. "In the end, Rebecca and I were not enough reason for her to want to live. She couldn't get beyond the loss of our son to see the two people who loved her and were still alive standing right in front of her."

Jesus, I can relate. His wife and my mom must be cut from the same cloth.

"She took her own life on the two-year anniversary of his death."

Shit. Such loss and devastation. "Why?"

He frowns and huffs in irritation.

"Why did this man kill your son?" I clarify.

"Ah, yes. You want to know how it all started." He stands, stretching. I can hear his back crack from across the room. He takes a deep breath, sliding easily from the heartbroken father and husband to the detached, angry killer I understand him to be. He leans back against my father's desk with his casual demeanor, but there is nothing laidback about this man.

I watch him wearily as he crosses his arms over his chest, his eyes scanning me in contemplative study. After what seems like forever, he begins to speak. "The man I'm searching for, my son's killer, upset a lot of bad people. People I owe, people I could not say no to. I was sent to make an example of him, show him and others like him there are far worse things than dying."

Shit. This is not good. This man is showing me who he really is, and I need to pay attention. I cannot afford to mess this up.

"He had two kids. A boy and a girl, almost the same age as mine. He had to choose one," he says in a cool tone.

"Choose one?" *Please don't say what I think you're going to say.*

"One of his kids was going to die. He had to choose which one. In front of his wife and children, he had to make a choice or they all died."

No.

"It wasn't easy, but finally he made his choice. He chose his daughter to die."

Fucking assholes, both of them, the one who chose and the one standing before me.

"You see, this was supposed to be a punishment of the greatest kind. He chose his son to live. Therefore, he was the one I killed."

Jesus. I grab onto the doorframe to steady myself, my knees weak and my stomach trying to convince me to throw up.

"No," I groan.

"In reality, he lost his whole family. His son died. His wife left him, and his daughter could never forgive him for choosing her to die. It was the worst kind of punishment. A living hell."

I swallow the bile rising in my throat. "He came after you. Made you make the same choice?"

He nods. "Yes, but I tried to outsmart him by choosing my son to die, thinking he would do the opposite, as I did, and kill my daughter. But he outsmarted me, and killed my son in front of my wife and daughter."

"Jesus, you all are a bunch of sick fucks. Using kids as chess pieces to get what you want, to manipulate the situation to your liking." I step into the room and pull the gun from my bra. My arm is steady, my aim is true. "No more. This ends here. I won't let anyone else die in the name of your sick game or those sick bastards you work for. I won't help you any longer. I'm not a pawn. I'm a living human being who has just as much right to live as you do, as your sons did."

If he's surprised I have a gun, he shows no hint of it. "Your father would be proud of you."

"Don't," I warn.

He just smiles and shakes his head. "I'm serious. I told him that day he should be proud of the strong woman you are."

"Stop! You won't manipulate me with your words."

He nods in understanding. "I want you to know, no matter how this ends, I meant what I said. I never meant to kill your father or harm you. What I have done in this life will haunt me into the next. I have made peace with that. But you do not want to taint yourself with the stain of taking another's life. You're too good for that."

"Sam." Michael calls from down the hall.

I don't take my eyes off of Roderick.

"Ah, good they're here." He motions to my gun. "You can put your gun down now. Let the professionals handle it from here." His voice is full of condescension, like I'm a good little girl, and I should run along home and let the adults handle this.

"Sam." Michael steps into the room, his weapon drawn and pointed at Roderick. "I've got this. Put the gun away and step down the hall."

I don't move. I don't look at Michael. I don't trust Roderick. It's too easy. He has something up his sleeve.

In a blink of an eye, Michael moves toward me, and Roderick reaches for the gun tucked in the waist of his pants.

"Look out!" I scream and squeeze the trigger just as Michael fires his gun.

Both shots hit Roderick square in the chest in a one-two punch, slamming him back against my dad's desk.

Blood stains the front of his shirt as he gasps for air.

The hand holding his gun falls slack at his side as he slides to the floor, landing on a thud and slowly keeling to one side.

I focus on his eyes that never seemed to leave mine, the life slowly draining away, reminding me of my father when he died. Even as the room fills with agents, and Michael puts his arm around me, guiding me from the room, Roderick's eyes stick to me like glue.

Twenty-One

Joseph

'M HAVING MY OWN GROUNDHOG DAY MOMENT here, getting a call telling me shots have been fired. My girl's in danger, and now I'm rushing to be by her side, not knowing if she's okay. I'm reliving the day her dad was killed and she was shot. And just like that day, nothing can keep me from her or my need to take her away from all this craziness.

I need her by my side, on my lap, in my arms, beneath me, however the fuck I can get her.

I. Need. Her.

The selfish caveman in me will not relent until that happens.

We pull up in front of her dad's office. Police cars, two ambulances, and a parking lot full of black unmarked cars—the FBI and Victor's team—clog my path.

Victor's on me before I make it ten steps and braces his hand against my chest. "She's fine. She's not hurt." He hedges as his hand drops from my chest. "At least not physically. Mentally, I would expect some residue."

Residue?

He grips my shoulders. "Joe, look at me. Focus."

I stop scanning the parking lot like a heat-seeking missile to concentrate on him.

"Roderick is dead," he says.

"Thank God." I let out a breath and relax. "What else?" I'm sure there's more, or he wouldn't be stopping me to tell me now, at this moment, when he knows all I want is to get to my girl.

"Both Michael and Sam shot him." His stern voice gentles.

"Fuck." I run my hands over my face and then through my hair. I'm filled with pride and sorrow. Pride for my girl kicking Roderick's ass and sorrow for how she might be feeling about it. I, for one, am happy he's gone and that she had something to do with it. A karmic *fuck you* to the motherfucker who killed her father.

I look back to him, but he's no longer watching me. I follow his sightline to Samantha sitting in the back of an open ambulance.

Mine, is all I can think as I make my way to her.

As soon as she sees me, she pushes the EMT aside and stands. "Joseph," she exclaims as she starts to run toward me.

It's like a fucking movie, her getting closer to me as though in slow motion. It's an eternity before her body crashes into mine on a leap, and she wraps her arms and legs around me and buries her head in my neck.

"Sweetness." I hold on to her, tightly. "Christ almighty, baby, I was so fucking scared. Never. Never do that to me again. No more guns, no more bad guys. Okay?"

"Joseph." She shakes as her sobs take over.

"Shh. It's okay, Sweetness. I got you." I close my eyes and sink into her neck, breathing her scent, her warmth. "God, I love you."

"I...I...looove...youuuu...too," she sobs.

My heart breaks for my girl. I can't ever let this happen again. Never. Ever.

Michael places a blanket over her shoulders. He nods at me, full of emotion himself, which only bodes for how heavy this whole thing is probably weighing on her.

"I want to talk to you," he says softly, glancing over his shoulder. "But I have to finish up here first." He looks at her and then me. "Maybe I can swing by, bring dinner. She's done what she needs to for now, anything else can wait. I'll get one of my guys to drive you home."

She relaxes in my arms, her sobs turning to sniffles. She's got to be as relieved as I am to not have to stick around.

He calls out to someone and then turns back to us, touching her back lightly. "You did good, Sam. I'm proud of you."

She slowly lifts her head, taking a second to wipe her nose and face with the blanket. She's disheveled and cute as hell with her red nose and pouty lips. Her legs release from around my waist, and I slowly lower her to the ground, holding her steady.

She surprises us both by barreling into Michael nearly as hard as she did to me, wrapping him in a hug. He quickly reciprocates. I stand there watching as they hug in silence.

They've spent a lot of time together. She trusts him with her life—she's had to. Luckily, that trust paid off. I clasp his shoulder. "Thank you for taking care of her, for all you've done for us. If you ever find you want a civilian job, come work for me at MCI. You'd work with Victor, but you'd be my man."

He gifts me with a rare smile. "You might regret that offer." He takes a second to examine the scene surrounding us. "It might be time for me to move on."

He squeezes Samantha and then steps back, meeting her eyes. "You need to get going. You'll crash soon. Have some food, lots of water, and then a nap. I'll see you later."

Samantha moves to my side, but her eyes stay on him. "You're a good friend, Michael. Thank you for protecting me."

When her gaze locks on mine with such love in her eyes, I could cry. *I'm a totally pussy when it comes to this girl.*

To Michael she asks, "Can you tell Scott and Sebastian too? Maybe y'all should come over for dinner, get it over with. I think once I go to bed tonight, I'm going to want to sleep for a week. I'd rather see everyone tonight and then have a few days with just Joseph." Her lovely face returns to me. "Are you okay with that?"

I kiss her temple. "Sounds perfect."

"Why don't we do it at my place, that way you two can leave when you feel like it." Fin's voice of reason comes from behind me.

"Thanks, Bro." That's a fucking fantastic plan.

With quick goodbyes and a promise to see them later, we make our escape.

I settle her in my arms in the backseat of a black SUV as Michael's man drives us home.

PART 9

MINE

Twenty-Two

Samantha

I FALL ASLEEP ON THE WAY THERE, ONLY WAKING UP at Joseph's gentle prodding once we're parked in the garage. We step into a different set of elevators on the wrong side of the building.

Home. When Joseph said home, I assumed he meant Fin's home. But apparently, he meant *his* penthouse in the adjacent tower of MCI, opposite from Fin and Matt's penthouses.

Noticing my confusion, Joseph hand circles my waist and tugs me into the elevator. "We're in the other tower. You're not staying with Fin any longer. You're staying with me." His expression is one of pure satisfaction.

"I need my things." I pull back, meaning to go to Fin's to collect them now instead of waiting. I'm starting to shut down. Once I stop moving, I'll crash. Hard.

He smiles and pulls me to his side as he secures the key and code to the penthouse level. "It's all taken care of, Sweetness."

"Oh." I'm relieved. Maybe I should be upset he just assumes I'll stay with him, but truly, I couldn't be happier.

As much as I pretend I don't, I like his caveman ways. He's an in-charge, take-charge kinda guy, and he suits me just fine. I feel cherished, seen, and appreciated. He wants me with him all the time. How could a girl not love that?

We step out of the elevator and into a vestibule identical to Fin and Matt's.

"How can you tell the difference?" I have a vision of being drunk and not having any idea which tower I'm in or which penthouse is his. I don't drink, but if I did, this could be a nightmare.

He laughs. "Well, besides the fact we came up a different set of elevators in a different tower, you can tell by the 2A next to our door. We're in 2A. The other building is the same except they're 1A, 1B, 1C, 1D. Fin is in 1A."

"How have I not noticed the numbers before?" I study the number at his door and then glance across the hall. Have the numbers been there the whole time? "I didn't know there were four more penthouses. Does this tower have a roof pool too?"

"Yes, and then two floors down is the fitness center." He frowns before he puts the key in the lock. "Did Fin never show you around?"

"No, I only knew about the pool because of Michael. Does the other building have a fitness center too?"

He smiles. "Tell you what. I'll take you on a tour tomorrow or the next day as soon as you feel up to it. I'll show you all the secret passageways and hidden doors this little key can get you into." His smirk is playful as he wags his brows at me.

I lean into him. "Sounds like fun."

He opens the door, and I'm momentarily brought back to the first time I entered Fin's penthouse. The lights turn on, seemingly on their own. These must be motion sensitive. I step through the entry and down into the living room. The space is exactly the same as Fin's except it has a different feel. This is homier, more laidback, more like Joseph. The same floor-to-ceiling windows take center stage as well as the wall-to-wall marble floors. I slowly approach the windows and notice this tower's penthouse faces the opposite direction. We have a more tranquil view of Reunion Tower, the Margaret Hunt Hill Bridge, and the Trinity River Corridor.

His warm body blankets me from behind as he wraps his arms around me. "What do you think?"

"It's beautiful, Joseph. I think I like this view better."

"Me too. I've always loved staying here. This one has the best view in my opinion."

"I would agree wholeheartedly." I lean into him, relishing this moment. I let out a long sigh when his lips press against my neck.

"Why don't you go take a hot bath and let me rustle up some lunch."

My stomach growls at that precise moment. We both laugh. "I think that sounds like a great plan." I kiss his cheek and start to head down the hall.

"Sweetness," he calls me to a halt.

I turn and face him. "Hmm?"

He smiles and saunters over to me, taking my hand and leading me in the other direction. "We're in the master suite."

"Oh." The thought never even crossed my mind. I was heading in the same direction as the guest room I occupied at Fin's.

If I wasn't so tired and sinking quickly, I would be totally impressed by the massive bedroom. The bathroom is larger than the one I used at Fin's, but the shower and bath fixtures seem to be identical, which is a good thing as it took me a while to master them.

Joseph starts the tub, dropping in a bath bomb, and turns to kiss me tenderly on the head. "Don't fall asleep, baby. I'll be back in a few with lunch."

After I'm settled and getting sleepy, he appears in the bathroom door holding a tray of goodies. "Nuh uh, don't fall asleep on me, Sweetness. I need to get you fed and to bed."

I sit up, hoping it'll revive me. "Sorry."

He sets down the tray and bends down to kiss my cheek. "Don't be. You've had a hard day."

Grabbing the vanity stool, he places it next to the tub. He sits down and begins to feed me bites of sandwich and fruit with sips of water in between. While I'm chewing he takes a bite and then feeds me more while he's chewing. *I think he likes to feed me.*

The whole interchange is quiet and relaxing. "You're a good caretaker, Joseph."

The entire time he stayed with me in the hospital and out, after I was shot, I don't think I ever said that to him. "You've always taken such good care of me. I'm sorry I've never told you before or said thank you. That was selfish of me. So, thank you."

"Samantha, it's my pleasure to take care of you." He brushes his cold watermelon lips across mine and pulls back with a smile. "Are you ready to get out?"

"Yes, I'm getting pruney."

He helps me out, wrapping a warm towel around me. He kisses my shoulder and leaves me to finish up as he jumps in the shower.

I finish drying off and slip on a silk robe, not bothering with panties. I don't know what Joseph has planned, but anytime I'm near him like this, intimately, not even necessarily sexually, my panties get soaked anyway, so what's the point? I quickly brush my teeth, avoiding his reflection in the shower or I'll never get out of here.

I grab our lunch tray and take it to the kitchen, cleaning up and then refilling our ice waters. As I pad back into the bedroom, it feels strange, like I'm going to Fin's bedroom. I'm sure I'll get used to it in time.

Joseph steps out of the bathroom as I enter the room. He frowns. "Why aren't you in bed?" Not chastising, just a question.

"I would have fallen asleep before you were done. I cleaned up lunch and refilled our waters." I hold up the glasses in my hands as evidence.

He walks over, taking them from me. "Thank you. Now get in bed." He's *Mr. Serious*.

I can't help but snicker as I drop my robe where I stand and walk to the bed buck naked. He merely groans behind me, and my smile only widens. I do manage to stifle it as I climb under the covers.

He sets down our waters and flicks off the lights before climbing in bed. Since it's early afternoon, some light creeps in through the curtains. They're blackout curtains, and it only took me one time to learn that when you close them completely, *blackout* means blackout. I couldn't see a damn thing. It was a little disconcerting and reminded me of visiting

Carlsbad Caverns as a kid, when they turned off all the lights for three of the longest minutes of my life. I was scared shitless and never wanted to go back. I appreciate the light and don't mind when some streams in, even when I'm trying to sleep.

"Come 'ere, Sweetness." He scoots closer, drawing me to his side, where I rest my head on his chest. He continues to situate me until we are completely touching down the length of our bodies.

I could do it myself, but it's kind of fun letting him. It thrills me that he wants me this close to him when we sleep. He's a cuddler, and he's not ashamed of it, not one bit. I love that about him.

He sighs and kisses my forehead. I know what's coming. What he's wanted since he found me at my dad's office. He needs me to unload on him, share the details of what happened, not leaving a single solitary thing out. It's as much for me as it is for him. He won't let me carry the burden of what I know alone. He wants to share it with me. He *needs* to share it. It kills him he couldn't be the one to be by my side, that it was Michael who was there in the end and not him. It was Michael's job, though, what he's trained to do. Joseph's guilt is misguided, believing he's lacking in some way, or worse—that he's let me down.

In my eyes, he wasn't lacking at all. He was where I needed him to be. Away from me, where he was safe, and I could concentrate on what needed to be done. I never could have kept my cool if Joseph had been there for me to rely on. I would have deferred to him and probably gotten us both killed. I needed to stand on my own two feet, and even as much as I did, I also knew he, Victor, and Michael's teams were there to back me up.

"Tell me, Sweetness. Tell me all of it." His voice deep and soothing, and I know I will never make it through this without more tears.

"I need you to forgive me for conspiring without you." I move back so my head rests on the pillow. I need to see his face. This incredibly handsome, masculine face showing how much I hurt him by keeping it from him. "I need you to forgive me for doing such a huge thing without you."

I touch his cheek. "I was so scared, Joseph." My tears start, and he wipes them away as they fall, one by one, and then a flood that is too copious to keep up with. "If things could have been okay without confronting him, I would have taken that path. But I knew, as all of you knew, that was never going to happen. He was never going to leave us alone as long as he held out hope we could give him the information he sought, or could use us to obtain it from someone else." My heart squeezes. "And that's why I pushed you away, distanced myself from you for so long. I couldn't bear the thought of anything happening to anyone else I love. I saw my dad…I couldn't bear to see that happen to you as well. I thought I was protecting you, but—"

"I know, Samantha. I'm not angry or disappointed in you. I know why you did it. I wish you'd let me help, but I understand why you thought you had to do it yourself." He presses his lips to mine. I close my eyes as his breath catches and his voice breaks. "I'm so fucking proud of you." He closes his eyes, and I break when tears streak down his face. It's my turn to wipe them away, kiss, and comfort.

"You couldn't do this for me, Joseph. I know you wanted to. You wanted to protect me from all of this, but you couldn't. I had to do what I needed to, to feel safe. I needed to be in control and not just a puppet. That's where Scott and Sebastian came in, and don't be mad at them. If they didn't help me, I would have done it without them. They didn't really have a choice. I didn't give them one. I suspected Scott was working with Victor because of a look I saw exchanged between the two of them, but they never thought I knew. That's why I had to keep my plan to disappear before the ceremony a secret. I wasn't even completely sure I was going to leave before my speech. I saw an opportunity and took it. Plus, I was impatient to get it over with. And not thrilled to be giving a speech in the first place," I confess.

I go on to share all of it with him, the details, my thoughts behind my actions and the horrible truth of why Roderick was after the guy who killed his son. When I finish, we both just lie there in silence. We'd long since switched to lying on our backs as I laid out what happened from the moment he left me behind the stage at the coliseum to when he found me sitting in the back of the ambulance.

"Christ, he was one messed up sonuvabitch. The whole situation was a nightmare. Do you think Michael knew the story between those two, about killing their sons?"

I shake my head. "I don't know. I would like to think he didn't, but I have no idea. You can ask him. I really don't want to think about it anymore. Once we meet with our families and everyone else tonight, and finish whatever needs to be done with the FBI, I just want to put it all behind me. Behind us."

He smiles. "I like that plan. Now, come 'ere. You need to rest, and I need to hold you."

He'll get no arguments from me. I cuddle back into his side, half-lying on him as his fingers lazily trace up and down my arm and hip in a slow, steady motion.

His tender touch and rhythmic breathing lull me to sleep, where I am safe and protected in the arms of the man I love.

Twenty-Three

Joseph

WE SPEND THE EVENING AT FIN'S, WELL, A COUPLE of hours at least. Samantha didn't seem up for more. All the hugs, congratulations, and emotions coming from everyone was a lot for her to take in. Even Jace was there to give his better-late-than-never support and love. I'm proud of him for that. He and I are nowhere near where we need to be, but I can see after today there's a good chance we'll get there.

Fin, Matt, and my parents, along with Michael, Victor, Scott, Sebastian, and Margot were all there. The guys joked with Samantha and Margot, telling them they needed to bring more X chromosomes to the next get-together. I would agree. There was entirely too much testosterone in that room. Though, the two of them did seem to eat up the attention, but I could see on Samantha's face they're a lot to take at one time.

Samantha and I say goodnight and make our way back to our penthouse via the elevators and crossover bridge.

Once inside, she lets out a deep sigh and rolls her neck and shoulders. The stress of today has gotten to her. I need to see what I can do to alleviate it.

I take her hand. "Let's get you to bed."

"I don't want to go to sleep."

"Who said anything about sleeping?" She gives a small squeal as I pick her up and make our way to our bedroom. "I believe I made you a promise, and I intend to keep it."

Her beautiful blue eyes are full of innocence. "Promise?"

I lay her down on our bed. "The promise that the moment you gave yourself to me, believed in our forever, believed in me, I was going to make you mine."

She shudders, and her warm palm captures my cheek, pulling me toward her. "I meant it when I sent you that text. I didn't say it because of what Jace told me about Tiff. I was all in before then."

I settle over her and kiss along her jaw to nuzzle her ear. "I know, Samantha. I read the letter you left for me." She shakes her head, so I clarify, "The what-if letter you left with Sebastian."

"Oh." Her forehead puckers. "You read it? I didn't mean for you to read it. Well, not unless something happened to me."

"Well, you addressed it to me, so I figured I had the right to read it either way." I study her remarkable face. What this woman does to me. "You wrote it before you talked to Jace." My voice cracks with emotion. "You gave yourself to me, not even knowing what really happened with Tiff. You forgave me thinking I had turned to another woman on the same night you broke up with me. You forgave me anyway."

Her letter was heartfelt, full of love and compassion and forgiveness for me. Believing I had chosen to sleep with someone else, she forgave me anyway—wanted to set me free of any guilt I may harbor. It wasn't long. It didn't hash out everything. She simply explained why she went behind my back to meet up with Roderick. She went on to apologize for leaving me in such a way and telling me how much she loved me and would haunt me until the day I died if I didn't mourn her sufficiently before I found my true love, married and had babies. She closed her letter telling me that I was the love of her life, and she only regretted not having a forever with me.

She smiles and kisses me softly. "I forgave you anyway. Always. That's what you do when you find your other half. You do whatever is necessary to be with them. Forgiving you was a small thing—you did nothing wrong. Forgiving myself?" She crinkles up her nose. "I'm working on it."

She touches my cheek. "Forgiving Jace. Not so much." She sighs and tries to sit up, but I stop her. "I'm so sorry, Joseph. What you went through, how you felt you needed to lie to protect Jace after what he did to you. I'm so upset with him. And you...you didn't know." She buries her face in my neck, sobbing. "I'm so sorry, Joseph. Please forgive me."

Christ. "Forgive you?" She feels guilty, like it's her fault. "I know I should be upset with Tiff, but honestly, I don't remember it, not in that way. What I remember is my fantasy of you. In my head and in my heart, it was you. No one else. She took advantage of the situation, and that was awful, but Tiff probably didn't know how gone I was. With Jace's encouragement and my body's reaction to her, she had no reason to believe I wasn't coherent enough to realize what was happening. It's disgusting, but the blame is on Jace for setting it all in motion. I don't know if Jace and I will ever overcome this, but no part of that is on you."

"But if I hadn't pushed you away—"

I pull back, needing to see her face. "You did nothing wrong. You were trying to keep me safe by keeping me away from you. We've both learned that together is where we're strongest. We know better now."

We stare at each other in silent communication, and then she nods, accepting my word as truth.

I bend closer. "Now, give me those lips, Sweetness, and let me make my fantasy a reality."

"Joseph." Her voice is so soft and reverent. I want to do everything I can to earn that from her every day of our lives.

"My beautiful girl, let me make love to you. Show you how it is between us, how it will always be." I steal a quick kiss before pulling away, needing her answer. "Be mine, Sweetness."

She sucks on my bottom lip, pulling slightly, and my cock draws to full staff. "I've always been yours, Joseph. From the first moment you laid eyes on me."

Christ, I love hearing her say she's mine. "Then let's make it official. Say yes."

"Yes," she says with the best smile and twinkle in her eyes.

"That's my girl," I groan seconds before my lips take hers.

We've kissed before, we've had months of kissing and touching, and even groping and sucking. But this right here, this first true kiss since she's agreed to be mine, is different. It's more precious than any kiss that has come before, even more than that very first one where she so impatiently told me she would burst for the waiting. This is the kiss marking she's truly mine. I will be the last man to ever kiss these sweet, luscious lips.

Mine.

Mine.

Mine.

I let it free, the caveman who needs to claim her for himself.

Breathlessly, I pull away. "I need you naked." She simply nods, and I stand up and start to strip. "I promise to go slower next time where I unwrap you like a present. But this time, I need to save my patience for when I'm actually inside you. I need to go slow, be gentle. I won't hurt you. I just don't have patience for clothing today."

Christ, I need to calm down. My heart is racing a million miles a minute. I need—want—this to be good for her. I want it to be everything.

She gives me a sweet smile as she stands up and starts to peel off her clothes. Once I'm naked, I pull back the covers and then turn to help with her bra and panties. She steals glances, but won't keep my eye contact. She's tentative, and I can't have that.

"Samantha." I cup her cheek and guide her eyes to mine. "I won't hurt you. I promise. If at any time you want me to stop, just say the word, and I will." I kiss her lips and all along her makeup-free face. I love her all made-up, but I love her all-natural best.

As she settles in our bed, I rein in my caveman who's screaming *take her* and decide on a new course, a slower one. I lie beside her, my body trembling with desire that's amped up due of the emotions of the day and the fact that this will be our first time—*her* first time.

I kiss her softly. "We're going to take this slow, okay?"

"You don't—"

"I do. I won't *take* your virginity. This is not about me *taking* anything from you. I want this to be about *giving*. I want to give you something no man ever has. I want to give you a part of me I've never given anyone. You're my heart, Samantha, and I need to cherish you, worship you, make love to you."

Her breath catches.

I kiss her pulse point on her neck, feeling her blood race. It's hot as fuck knowing how turned on she is. Chin tilted, she gives herself to me. "So sexy."

She moans as my fingers trace along each breast, circling but never touching her nipples. I kiss along her neck and make my way back up to her lips. "My beautiful girl."

Every time I speak she lets out a sigh. I love how I affect her. For every squirm, moan, sigh, arch, and shudder, I feel it too. Her pleasure is my pleasure. Her racing heart and heady desire meets my racing heart and heady desire. She gives back to me in every breath of her being, in every touch of her warm, needful hands, and in the wanton haze in her eyes.

My girl.

As I play with her nipples, her arching back tells me what she really wants. With a lingering kiss, I slowly nip, suck, and kiss my way down her neck and chest to her stiff, succulent peaks. "So fucking beautiful."

She cries out as I tease and suck on her nipples. My cock, painfully hard, rubs against her thigh.

Her hands have free rein and alternate between imploring, guiding, and exploring.

"Joseph," she begs.

"I know, baby." I know what she needs, where she needs me.

My hand makes a path down her body, taking time to enjoy every inch of her silky skin. She nearly jerks off the bed when I graze over the soft spot just above her hip bone.

She catches herself and giggles. "Sorry." Her smile is sheepish and embarrassed.

I grin and kiss her swollen lips. "Don't be." My hand continues down, down, until I reach my destination. I watch her face as I slide my palm over her mound. Her mouth opens as a sigh escapes, and her body rocks into my touch. Her head tilts back, but her eyes never leave mine as she continues to glide slowly against my hand, back and forth. "Christ, Sweetness. I think I could come just from watching you rub against my hand."

"Yeeeessss…come." She groans, and I nearly fucking do.

I don't know how much more of this I can take, but I'm lost in her, lost in her pleasure, lost in her seductive shyness and the way she gives herself over to me. I'm so lost that I'm found.

My middle finger slips between her folds, easily slipping through her wet heat. Her hips call me, beckon me, draw me into her. And I do, I go where I've never gone before with her. As soon as I'm inside her, she arches back, and her inside contract around my finger, pulling at me, drawing me in. Beautiful and…tight.

Christ, so tight. I'm going to die when I finally get my cock inside her.

I realize now I shouldn't have waited to do this. I should have been doing this all along, getting her ready, stretching her to accommodate my size. I don't want to hurt her.

I freeze.

"Joseph, what's wrong?"

"You're tight. I'm afraid I'll hurt you."

She pulls my face to hers. "It might hurt at first, but it's okay. It's to be expected, right? You didn't really think my first time would be painless, did you?"

I shake my head. "I'd hoped it could be." I see the disbelief on her face. "I've never had sex with a virgin. I've never been anyone's first choice." I didn't realize how much that meant to me until I said those words out loud.

"Joseph, you are my first choice for everything, but especially this." She pulls my hand away and pulls me on top of her. "Now kiss me and make love to me. Enough waiting. I think I will surely burst if I have to wait for you any longer."

Her playful pouting is adorable. "God, I love you."

She nods. "I know. Now show me." She wraps her legs around mine and swats my ass.

I chuckle. "You're going to be the death of me, aren't you?"

"I sure hope not." She smiles deviously. "Kiss me."

My fear of hurting her has taken the edge off my urgency. I can do this. Our lips meet in a heated caress, just as my cock rests against her pussy. As I slip my tongue inside her mouth, she arches and rocks her hips against me, and the tip of my cock slips inside her. She gasps, not in a painful way, but in an oh-my-god-that-feels-amazing way.

With the catch of her breath and the arch of her hips, I slip in further.

Tight. So tight.

I rest my forehead against hers. "You okay?" *Please, be okay.*

She rocks against me, again. "Yes, Joseph."

She arches back. "Please," she moans.

Fuck. That's it.

I push in further. Slowly, with each rock of her hips I sink deeper until I am fully seated inside the warmest, tightest, most succulent pussy I've ever felt.

She will absolutely be the fucking death of me.

"Oh god, Joseph." Her sexy voice reaches my ears right as she squeezes my cock and comes.

I've barely even moved, and she's coming all over me. I groan as I watch, feeling her tremble and moan my name. The most beautiful sight and sound I've ever witnessed.

"Fucking spectacular, Sweetness." I kiss along her neck and face, and gently peck at her lips until she comes back from her orgasmic high.

Her eyes open, and a radiant smile spreads across her lips. "Wow."

I nod. "Yeah, wow." I suck her bottom lip and then pull back. "Now, let's do that again, and this time I'm coming with you."

"Yes, please."

I chuckle at my sweet sexy girl. So full of wonder and passion. Will I ever get my fill?

Not.

A.

Fucking.

Chance.

Twenty-Four

Samantha

JESUS, THERE'S BLOOD EVERYWHERE. I CAN'T GET IT *to stop.* "Daddy!"

"It's okay, pumpkin." *His hand cups my cheek, grounding me.* Breathe. Don't think about the blood.

His eyes shine with tears, and his skin pales—fading. "Don't be afraid," *he whispers through a wisp of a smile.* "Love. You."

"Daddy," *I sob.* "I love you, too." *My words fall on deaf ears.*

"I love you, too." *I cry to the heavens because that's the only way he'll hear me.*

I bolt awake, a sob on my lips, a knife in my heart, and gasping for air. "Fuck." I exhale as I realize it was only a dream. A nightmare. A memory.

His arms surround me on my next breath. "Sweetness." His warmth draws out the painful memories and combats my sorrow.

"Joseph." I bury my face in his neck. "My dad…" is all I manage before my tears take over, any semblance of composure gone.

"I know. You cried out for him." He squeezes me tighter. "Shh. I got you, Samantha. It's over. It's all over." His gravelly voice, sexy and calming, covers me like warm memories and happily-ever-afters.

Daddy, I'm not afraid anymore. I wonder if he can hear me.

I peer up at Joseph. His beautiful face is distorted with sympathy and eyes glistening with tears. I wipe my eyes and sniffle, trying to find solid ground through the latent haze of my dream and the reality staring me in the face.

"That day, he told me not to let fear stand in my way of seeing what's right in front of me. To not let my mature ways squash what remains of my childish hope and belief so I could see the life I could have with you."

A single tear falls from his soulful green eyes, watching me, waiting.

"I'm sorry it took me so long to see it, to believe in it, to believe in us."

"Sweetness." His lip trembles and tears fall, and my heart races, pounding with need to make this right.

"I believe, Joseph. I believe in you. I was just afraid." My voice cracks on the last word as his lips press to mine.

"No more fear, baby. Not about us."

"No more," I agree, kissing him back.

Our mouths make peace with the turmoil that's been between us, on and off since we met.

"No more," I breathe against his lips.

He smiles and kisses down my jaw to my earlobe, nipping it gently before rasping in my ear. "I need more of you."

His breath sends a shudder through my body and moisture to my core. "Yes," I hiss, and latch on to his shoulder as he rolls us to my back.

Hot kisses traverse my body, licking and sucking in rapturous consumption of every inch of my skin. I'm on fire with desire and arching with need, aching for him.

"Joseph." It's a plea, an exultation, a demand.

Tight, hot, and shaking with restraint, Joseph, enters me on a groan so feral, goosebumps ripple across my body. I wrap round him, consuming his scent, his sounds, his beauty in motion.

"Fuck, yes," he chants on every pump of his hips, not gentle, not rough, just achingly perfect.

I try to concentrate on him, watch his single-minded focus as he makes love to me, but it's a lost cause. With every thrust, I cry out, lost in my own pleasure, rising higher and higher.

"So beautiful, Sweetness," he murmurs against my mouth, before sucking on my bottom lip as he pinches my nipple.

"Oh." *Jesus.* I clamp down as the jolt of pleasure sears to my clit. "Again."

He growls as he does it again.

"Oh, god. Joseph…I'm gonna—"

"Come," he finishes for me.

That jolt of pleasure turns into an outright explosion, my words lost on the moan that rips through me as my body takes flight.

"Fuck." His arms wrap around me. His hips surge deeper, grinding round and around, pistoning through every tremor. "Christ, Samantha, I love the way you squeeze me when you come."

His words and the groan he lets loose as he comes send me into another orgasm even stronger than the first. I'm lost, soaring above, tethered only by his hold on me and the sensation of him coming inside me.

"Sweetness," he coos against my neck as I come down from my blissful high and the last of my orgasmic contractions wane.

Kisses rain across my face, my body going limp, still holding on to him, but just barely.

"God, I love you." I breathe out on a sigh of release.

I had no idea sex could be this good.

This spectacular.

He's a god.

And he's *mine.*

He chuckles, brushing my hair from my face. "I love you too, sweets."

Rolling to his side, he situates me the way he likes. "Now, go to sleep, Samantha." He kisses my temple. "You're keeping me from my beauty sleep."

I swat at his chest as he chuckles, thinking he's so funny. *Ass.*

He captures my hand and presses it to his lips. "What? You don't need beauty sleep, Sweetness. There's nothing on this earth that could make you any more beautiful to me."

Shit. Okay, he's a sweet ass.

I cuddle into him and let out a sigh of contentment, the stress of the day leaving on that puff of air. My body relaxes further with every soothing stroke of his hands, beat of his heart, and brush of his lips.

"Sleep, baby," he whispers before I finally let go and succumb to the night.

Joseph

I made love to her three times last night, and she came multiple times, each and every time. My inflated ego was undaunted by her teasing me over breakfast, telling me it was the best sex she's ever had. Of course, I'm the *only* sex she's ever had, and I plan to keep it that way.

I tell her she's the best sex I've ever had, hands down. Sadly, she's not the only sex I've ever had, but she wipes all others from my mind. With her, I have a clean slate, and I intend to fill up every inch of that slate with her pleasure.

I kiss her softly. "Are you sore, Sweetness?" My cock hardens as to the why she'd be sore.

Her sweet smile warms my heart as she leans her head on my shoulder. "Only in the most delicious of ways."

After she finishes her last bite of breakfast, I whisk her back to our bedroom. I can't keep my hands off her or my dick out of her now that I've had her. Maybe it was the waiting, maybe it's the love, maybe it's her. Actually, I'm quite positive it's her. I've never loved anyone like I love her, nor have I ever wanted someone like I want her, not just sexually either. I need her in my everyday life. I need a life partner, and she is it for me.

If I didn't think she'd freak out, I'd ask her to marry me right here, right now while I'm inside her. But, she's not ready for that. She just got on board the Joseph and Samantha Train, and I'm not doing anything to derail it. Though, I'm going to do all I can to keep us on the same track, heading in the same direction. Together.

After, I kiss her head, cuddled into our post-coital position, her back to my front. "You know I'm never going to let you out of this bed, right?"

She giggles. "I'm starting to see that." She squeezes my arm around her waist. "I'm not complaining. I love being here in your place, in your bed. I had misgivings about you living in a penthouse, but I'm beginning to see the appeal."

"Not my place, not my bed. This is *our* place, *our* bed. Unless you'd rather we live someplace else?" I nuzzle into her neck. Her softness and scent are making me hard, again.

She sighs. "No, I love it right here."

I grind my erection against her ass. "I'm going to make love to you all summer."

She shudders in my arms, and her nipple hardens under my palm.

"Mmm, you like that, Sweetness."

I tweak her nipple, and instinctively her ass presses into me. "Joseph."

My lips run up the curve of her shoulder as I continue to taunt her with my hands. "We may never even make it to MCI this summer. I don't think I can stop wanting—needing—to be buried deep inside you long enough for either of us to go to work."

I pull her top leg over mine and push into her slowly from behind. She arches and gasps, making my cock harder than ever. "It feels better every time. How is that even possible?" I snap my hips and fill her completely.

"Oh, god," she moans and reaches down, grabbing my ass, sinking her fingers into me with every thrust.

"Then when we move to Austin, you're gonna live with me,

Sweetness. I'm not ever going to let you out of my bed. I don't care if we live in the same house with Jace or find someplace new, but you and me are it. There's no more living apart from each other, not for a night, not for a week. Not ever."

My right hand moves down her body, slipping into her wet folds, finding her clit swollen and ready. My cock pushes into her over and over from behind, the motion rubbing her clit across my fingers.

She's close already, her warm pussy squeezing me so tightly. "Tell me you want that, Samantha." Her walls clench around me, letting me know she does, but I need to hear her say it.

"Yes, Joseph. All of it, yes."

Thank fuck. "Now come for me, my sweet. Take me with you."

I bite into her neck, sucking and licking the spot that sets her off and fulfills my caveman need to mark her. A need that will probably continue until she is mine in every sense of the word.

When she detonates, I hold on for the ride of my life as I take her pleasure and give her all of mine, pumping my seed deep inside her. "My Sweetness."

My girl.

My love.

My life.

My forever.

The End

Acknowledgements

Thank you to my husband for his unwavering support. It means the world to me that he's proud of me and my accomplishments. To my children who make me feel like I'm conquering the world with each word I write. You are my heart—I do this for you. To my mom, thank you for loving me when it wasn't easy and for supporting me in my passion.

Special thanks to Teddy for sharing this writing journey with me. I truly don't believe I would have made it this far without her undying support, knowledge, and sisterhood-of-the-traveling-pants type of connection we have.

To Tamara, who kicks my ass when my story needs it and for sticking with me as my editor. I live for her praise, like the needy little writer I am.

To my follow writerly peeps: Teddy, Shelly, Gayla – thanks for all the support and putting up with my Thursday Inspiration, Friday Humor, and Hottie McHottie emails. I enjoyed each and every one nearly as much as I enjoy you.

And lastly, to the readers—thank you for sticking with me through the cliffhanger in book 1, *Until You Set Me Free* (dmckdavis.com/books/until-you-set-me-free). I promise to *try* not to have any more of those, but sometimes the characters have so much to say, it's hard to get it all in just one book. I'm even more in love with Joseph and Samantha by the end of book 2. I pray you want more as their love story continues in *Until You Say I Do* (dmckdavis.com/books/until-you-say-i-do). That is the last from them, at least for now, but you will continue to see them in Fin's story—Until You Believe (dmckdavis.com/all-books/series/until-you/uybelieve).

Until next time, I will continue to write...

"What only the heart hears..."

About the Author

D.M. Davis is a Contemporary and New Adult Romance Author.

She is a Texas native, wife, and mother. Her background is Project Management, technical writing, and application development. D.M. has been a lifelong reader and wrote poetry in her early life, but has found her true passion in writing about love and the intricate relationships between men and women.

She writes of broken hearts and second chances, of dreamers looking for more than they have and daring to reach for it.

D.M. believes it is never too late to make a change in your own life, to become the person you always wanted to be, but were afraid you were not worth the effort.

You are worth it. Take a chance on you. You never know what's possible if you don't try. Believe in yourself as you believe in others, and see what life has to offer.

Please visit her website, dmckdavis.com, for more details, and keep in touch by signing up for her newsletter, and joining her on Facebook, Twitter, and Instagram.

Additional Books by
D.M. DAVIS

Until You Series

Book 1—Until You Set Me Free

Book 2—Until You Are Mine

Book 3—Until You Say I Do

Book 4—Until You Believe

Finding Grace Series

Book 1—The Road to Redemption

Book 2—The Price of Atonement

Black Ops MMA Series

Book 1—No Mercy

Book 2—Rowdy

Book 3—Captain

Standalones

Warm Me Softly

Join My Reader Group

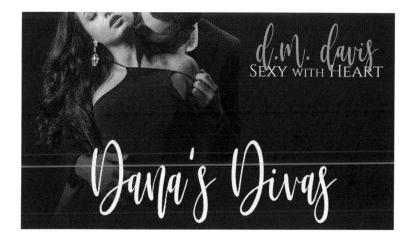

www.facebook.com/groups/dmdavisreadergroup

Stalk Me

Visit www.dmckdavis.com for more details about my books.

Keep in touch by signing up for my Newsletter.

Connect on social media:
Facebook: www.facebook.com/dmdavisauthor
Instagram: www.instagram.com/dmdavisauthor
Twitter: twitter.com/dmdavisauthor
Reader's Group: www.facebook.com/groups/dmdavisreadergroup

Follow me:
BookBub: www.bookbub.com/authors/d-m-davis
Goodreads: www.goodreads.com/dmckdavis

d.m. davis
SEXY WITH HEART
CONTEMPORARY & NEW ADULT ROMANCE AUTHOR

Printed in Great Britain
by Amazon

32042329R00133